MURDER AT
PLIMOTH
PLANTATION

MURDER AT

PLIMOTH

PLANTATION

LESLIE WHEELER

THE LARCOM PRESS, PRIDES CROSSING, MA

2001

The Larcom Press
P.O. Box 161
Prides Crossing, Massachusetts 01965
www.larcompress.com

Cover by Leeann Leftwich.

Printed in the United States on permanent paper.

The Larcom Press™ and A Larcom Mystery™ are trademarks.

Permissions

Excerpts from *Of Plymouth Plantation 1620-1647* by William Bradford,
edited by Samuel Eliot Morison, Copyright © 1952 by Samuel Eliot
Morison and renewed 1980 by Emily M. Beck. Used by permission of
Alfred A. Knopf, a division of Random House, Inc.

Grateful acknowledgment is also made to Applewood Books, Bedford,
Massachusetts, for permission to quote excerpts from *Mourt's Relation,
A Journal of The Pilgrims at Plymouth,* edited with an introduction and
notes by Dwight B. Heath from the original text of 1622, copyright ©
1963 Dwight B. Heath; and from *Good Newes from New England, a
True Relation of Things Very Remarkable at the Plantation of Plimoth
in New England* by Edward Winslow, first published in 1624.

ISBN 0-9678199-7-0

First Edition

In memory of my mother,
Helene Albright Wheeler

ACKNOWLEDGMENTS

My visits to Plimoth Planation were always informative and fun. From the many conversations I had with interpreters and other staff, I came away with a tremendous appreciation of the hard work and dedication that goes into presenting the Pilgrims to contemporary audiences. Stephen Eddy Snow's book, *Performing the Pilgrims: A Study of Ethnohistorical Role-Playing at Plimoth Plantation*, provided me with important insights about the nature of first-person interpretation and its development at Plimoth Planation.

I am grateful to my teacher, Barbara Shapiro, in whose mystery-writing class at the Cambridge Center for Adult Education this book began, for encouraging me to continue beyond the first chapter. I am also grateful to the members of my writers' critique group, past and present: Mark Ammons, Gena Corea, Kathy Fast, Margaret Leibenstein, Paula Messina, and Barbara Ross, for their patient reading of the various drafts and their many helpful suggestions.

Thanks go also to my agent, John Talbot, for his unflagging enthusiasm, and to Susan Oleksiw and Ann Perrott of The Larcom Press for making available a small-press alternative to New England mystery writers like myself.

Others who helped in different ways were Peter Keville, who told me the story of his Pilgrim ancestor, John Howland; Nancy Spence, who spent time location scouting with me on the South Shore; Sumner Silverman and Sally

Pierce, who hosted me on Martha's Vineyard; Joyce Lautens
O'Brien, who offered advice and encouragement along the
way; and my sister, Susan Wheeler Rappe, who reminded me
of our family's *Mayflower* connection and got me to Plimoth
Plantation for the first time. Finally, I wish to thank my husband, Robert A. Stein, and my son, Nicholas Leonard
Wheeler Stein, for their love and support.

MURDER AT
PLIMOTH
PLANTATION

1

"...you are many of you strangers, as to the persons, so to the infirmities one of another, and so stand in need of more watchfulness this way, lest when such things fall out in men and women as you suspected not, you be inordinately affected with them...." *Mourt's Relation*

He had to die.

I knew that from the start. I also knew that by the time I left Ferdinand Magellan bleeding on the beach in the Philippines, his body stuck through with Indian arrows, I'd be a wreck. A hazard of my work as a writer of textbooks like this one—*America, the Republic's Glory and Greatness* (*ARGG* when I was annoyed)—was that I lived what I wrote. A marathon at the computer left me with as much energy as a Himalayan climber in the final stage of hypothermia.

Nine P.M. If I pushed, I could put in three more hours before calling it a night. But I'd need fresh coffee.

The coffee maker burbled. Before I plunged into the past, was there any current business that needed attention? I followed a trail of Post-its scattered like confetti around my apartment—on the refrigerator, a reminder to buy milk; by the light switch, one to pay Com Electric; near the trash bin, a note to take out the garbage—my nose could have told me that!

In the bedroom I paused to examine a photograph on the dresser. A little girl in a lavender sweat suit and pink sneakers beamed at me. Her nose was a shiny red button, pink circles decorated her cheeks, and cardboard reindeer antlers crowned her strawberry blonde hair. What a cutie. I felt a rush of affection, then a guilty twinge.

Now eighteen, my niece Caroline was taking time off between high school and college to work as a first-person interpreter at Plimoth Plantation, portraying a Pilgrim woman who'd lived three hundred years ago. For Caroline the job was the realization of a long-cherished dream.

On a sweltering August day ten years ago, my ex-husband, Simon, and I had taken Caroline—dragged was more like it, since she'd protested all the way—to Plimoth Plantation for the first time. We had to bribe her with the biggest Slush Puppy we could buy just to get her up the path to the village. Even then it was hardly love at first sight. Accustomed to the air-brushed charms of Disneyland, she found the village with its crude houses and dusty main street stupid and bor-ring, her two favorite adjectives for anything she didn't like. When we finally coaxed her inside one of the houses and a Pilgrim woman spoke to Caroline in the quaint English of her forebears, the whiny eight-year-old was transformed into a rapt listener.

From that moment on she was hooked. She begged us to take her back to Plimoth Plantation the next day. And the day after and the day after that. By the end of her visit with Simon and me, she'd abandoned her ambition of becoming a world-famous ballerina in favor of becoming a Pilgrim interpreter. She'd given her parents no peace until reluctantly they agreed to let her have her wish—at least for a season.

But for her overly protective mother, Caroline's dream job was a transcontinental nightmare. Once a month, my sister-in-law, Eileen, had jetted in from California for several days until grounded by a peculiarly twentieth-century malady, a virulent strain of "airplane air" flu. While she recovered, I was supposed to be picking up the slack. But lately with *ARGG* deadlines looming, the rope had slipped from my hands.

Plimoth Plantation was only an hour's drive from Cambridge, yet I hadn't visited in five weeks. I hadn't telephoned either. The "call Caroline" Post-it attached to the phone had faded from a sunny yellow to the ghastly hue of a pre-tornado sky. I'd be seeing Caroline on Thanksgiving, a week from today. But a call now would ease my conscience.

"Oh . . . Miranda . . . hi." The words came out haltingly and Caroline's normally upbeat voice betrayed a tremor. On her mother's Richter scale, it would've been considered a major quake; on mine it barely registered. Still, it was worth checking out.

"Everything okay, Caro? You sound a little down."

"I'm fine."

"You're sure?"

"I just—" She broke off, made gulping sounds.

"What is it? You can tell me."

"Can't!" The floodgates burst. Click. Buzz.

So much for easing my conscience.

I slammed on the brakes. An instant later, I'd have collided with a red Jeep Cherokee roaring into the parking lot at Plimoth Plantation.

"You oughta have your license lifted!" a man yelled.

I gave him the finger, or rather something more like the peace sign. Rattled, I become a klutz. It was a bad move. The Jeep driver jumped out. He was big enough to make me, at five feet, nine inches, feel petite. He wore work boots, jeans, a down vest over a plaid flannel shirt, and a backwards baseball hat. Reflector sunglasses hid his eyes, giving him a sinister look. He leaned on the door frame of my car and thrust his broad face at the window. "Watch where you're going!"

"Don't drive so fast," I retorted.

"I'm late."

"So? I've got troubles of my own."

He rolled back on the balls of his feet, surveying me and my rusty, none-too-trusty Peugeot. "I can see that." A smile tugged at the corners of his mouth. Maybe he was all bark.

My reflection flashed at me from his mirrored sunglasses. A middle-aged Little Orphan Annie with a tangle of red hair and three foolishly upraised fingers. "What's your big rush?" I demanded.

"That." He gestured toward a group of placard-wielding Native Americans milling in front of the barnlike Visitor Center.

"You're one of them?"

"*The one.* I'm the guy who put it all together," he boasted. Evidently his ego matched his size.

"Hey, Nate, get your ass over here!" a demonstrator yelled.

"Gotta go. Don't want the brothers thinking I'm sleeping with the enemy."

"You—" Flushing with anger, I started to give him the finger again, but with a grin and a wave he was gone. I took a few moments to cool off before heading toward the Visitor Center myself.

As I approached the demonstrators, I glanced at their signs. "Pilgrims, Go Home." "No Thanksgiving for Native Peoples." "Plimoth—the Place Where It All Ended."

Could this demonstration be the cause of Caroline's distress? Possibly. If she had a fault, it was that she took things too much to heart. I, on the other hand, had seen my share of protests during the sixties in California and later in politically correct Cambridge. I found nothing remarkable about this one.

But wait a minute. "Myles Standish Is a Murderer"? The words in dripping red paint leaped off the placard. I stopped short, struck by both the specificity and severity of the charge. This was revisionist history in which a saint turned out to be a scoundrel. But was it true? I was an historian, I should know. And why "Is a Murderer" as if Standish killed someone recently?

The sign holder was a young Native American with a distinctive haircut, close-shaven around the sides and arranged into two braids at the crown. I stared at him a nanosecond too long and broke the first rule of dealing with threatening situations: avoid eye contact.

The Native American called Nate stepped forward. "You gotta problem?" No trace of teasing now. He was back to being leader of the pack.

Another showdown with this big man with a big attitude was the last thing I needed. I gave him my sweetest smile. "No problem."

Inside the Visitor Center, bedlam reigned. Every elementary school within a fifty-mile radius of Plymouth must have chosen the Friday before Thanksgiving for its field trip. Not the best time for me to visit, but what else could I do? Caroline had refused to answer the phone last night and again this morning. Something was up. I wanted to take care of it before her parents flew in for Thanksgiving.

Schoolchildren swirled noisily around me. I wrote textbooks for kids like these, but until now I'd successfully avoided them. I felt as comfortable as an agoraphobe at a rock concert. Flashing my membership card at the frazzled woman behind the entrance desk, I snagged a map and fought my way through heavy foot traffic up the paved path leading to the Pilgrim village.

At the crest of the hill, a red-lettered sign with a Pilgrim woman welcomed me to the seventeenth century. Another sign advised me to leave my twentieth-century trash in the receptacle provided. The weathered, white oak timbers of the palisade and the peaked roof of the Fort/Meetinghouse loomed ahead. I paused at the open gate as schoolchildren stampeded past.

In the world I was about to enter the seasons changed, but the year was always the same: 1627. The people who lived here spoke a different language, adhered to a different reality. In this *Twilight Zone*, my niece was not Ms. Caroline Lewis, a carefree teenager from La-La land. She was Mistress Fear Allerton, daughter of Elder William Brewster, religious leader of the Separatist congregation, and at twenty-one, the mother of a young child and a woman with important duties and responsibilities as the wife of Master Issac Allerton, business agent for the Pilgrims.

"What the hell's going on, Caro?" would elicit only a blank stare. I'd have to say something like, "What ails thee, mistress?" and hope for a less-than-cryptic reply.

Beyond the village, I glimpsed the slate-blue waters of Cape Cod Bay and the finger of land called Gurnet Point. A blast of icy air buffeted me. I shivered and tugged at the zipper of my parka. Head bent against the wind, I made a beeline for the palisade gate.

"We're going to fire the cannon at you!" A gaggle of children grinned down at me from slits in the second story of the Fort/Meetinghouse. Their compatriots swarmed below. Shouting and shrieking, they dashed in and out of the crude wattle-and-daub houses, chased chickens wandering loose in the sandy streets, trampled the gardens behind the houses, and tried to climb into the pens with sheep, goats, and pigs.

"Boys, we're not going to just run through this place," a harried chaperone called. "Remember, we're looking for the names of the people who live here." Thank heaven I'd chosen textbook writing instead of classroom teaching!

An SRO crowd packed the single whitewashed room of the Allerton house. I barely squeezed in. Smoke from the fire burning in the hearth filled the air, making my eyes water and threatening asphyxiation. But seemingly unaware of this health hazard, a Pilgrim woman stood at a rectangular table covered with an Oriental rug. She wore a dark green woolen gown with a white ruffled collar and skirts so voluminous that at least half the kids in the room could have hidden under them. A white coif concealed all but a few strands of her strawberry blonde hair. Children with turkey-shaped name tags pressed close, gaping as she stuffed ground meat into sausage casing. I suppressed the urge to remind her of the safe-handling instructions for pork. The children, however, had no such compunction. While I fretted, a boy tried to poke his finger into the pork. The woman caught his finger and whisked it away. "Have a care, lad, this sausage be not yet cooked and when 'tis, it be intended for our bellies, not yours."

I felt a swell of pride as if I'd trained her for the part myself, then curiosity. Was this calm professional the same person who'd burst into tears and hung up on me last night? Maybe my concern was misplaced after all. I edged closer. Caroline saw me and a red flush shot up her neck like mercury in a thermometer. She glanced quickly away. Maybe not.

"What's your name?" a girl with glasses asked, pencil poised over a piece of paper held against another girl's back.

"Mistress Fear Allerton."

"How'd you get a name like Fear?" glasses demanded.

"I be named for a virtue: Fear of the Lord."

"Do you have kids?" the girl whose back served as a writing board chimed in.

"Aye, child, in the pen outside."

"You keep them in a pen?"

" 'Tis the best place for our young goats."

A few children snickered, the rest simply stared. I was jostled from behind. Another group was trying to get in.

"Let's give the others a chance," their teacher said.

They started filing out. I moved in on Caroline, close enough to see the pale freckles dotting her fair skin like flecks in buttermilk. The flush had spread into her face, giving it a mottled look.

"Miranda, you didn't have to—"

"Of course, I did," I whispered. "We need to talk."

"Not now." She frowned at the doorway.

"When? Ouch!" A clipboard banged my elbow. The next onslaught was in full swing. Children pushed between us.

"I be going to my husband i' th' fields at nooning, mistress," Caroline informed me.

This was code for her lunch break. I looked at my watch. Eleven-thirty. I had a half hour to kill.

Outside, I glanced around. Was there someone else I could sound out about Caroline? A heavyset Pilgrim with a hangdog face sat on a bench in front of the next house down, or rather hovel—it was little more than a hole in the ground covered with a thatched roof. He whittled a piece of wood, watching it shrink with such a doleful expression that it might have been his diminishing hopes. According to my map, the hovel belonged to John Billington and his wife, Elinor, one of the few families to survive the ordeal of the first winter, in which disease and starvation claimed many among the *Mayflower* passengers. Maybe it was the memory of that awful time that made him look so melancholy. Or maybe it had to do with the fact that, as my map informed me, he was often at cross purposes with the Pilgrim leaders. In any case, I didn't know the man who played John Billington. Nor, for that matter, was I well acquainted with many of Caroline's fellow interpreters.

The one I knew best was Beryl Richards. A cohead of the interpretive program, she wasn't just Caroline's boss, but a kind and understanding person who'd taken my niece under her wing. She might have a clue about what was bothering Caroline. The only trouble was I couldn't remember which part she played. I thought her Pilgrim surname began with a *B*. But was she Elinor Billington, resident of yon hovel and missus to Mr. Hangdog? Or Alice Bradford, wife of Plimoth's august governor, whose house stood directly across the street? I decided to try the Bradford house.

The governor's better half was out, but he was there, seated at a table with an open book before him. Instead of reading, he was speaking with a passel of schoolchildren. He glanced up when I entered. A gaunt, rawboned man with a beaked nose and a shock of graying hair, he was Ichabod Crane in Pilgrim dress. I recognized him as Seth Lowe, the other head of the interpretive program.

I started to back out, but he beckoned me to remain. "Nay, mistress, be not shy. I be telling these children 'bout th' great brabble we had wi' th' naturals to the north—those that call themselves th' Massachusetts—an' how they did conspire to ruinate us. Ere they could do so, Captain Standish an' eight others went to a place called Wessagussett 'pon pretext o' trade an' cut down several o' their number."

So Myles Standish had been a murderer of sorts. These kids must've seen the same sign I had and asked about it.

"What'd they do to the Indians, scalp' em?" a boy in a Goosebumps sweatshirt demanded.

"Nay, lad, they did only what Englishmen in London do to those who commit treason. They cut off th' head o' a great villain called Wituwamat—one who had mocked us afore, saying th' English died crying, more like children than men—an' brought it back on a pike. This they did place 'pon th' battlements as a warning to other naturals o' like mind."

"Where's the skull now?" Goosebumps asked, wide-eyed.

" 'Twas there grinnin' down from a fence post when last I looked," Bradford replied with a wink at me. "Did ye not see it?"

The children rushed out to check. Now was my chance to ask about Beryl Richards's whereabouts. But before I could do so, a commotion erupted outside. "Mayhap they have found th' skull," Bradford said. I went to investigate.

At the bottom of the hill, a crowd had gathered. Two boys straddled the top of the palisade, war-whooping and menacing their fellows below. "Down from the fence, lads!" commanded a Pilgrim. He wore a helmet, gorget, breast-plate, and cape and carried a musket. The boys ignored him. "If ye will not come willingly, I must needs use force." He waved his musket at them.

"Shoot 'em down! Shoot 'em down!" the kids on the ground clamored, grabbing at the musket. The man raised it out of reach. "Shoot! Shoot!" they cried.

I glanced at Caroline's house, thinking she might've come out to see what was going on. She hadn't, but I noticed that John Billington, the hangdog Pilgrim, had stopped whit-tling and was watching, open-mouthed with an expression of alarm.

The gun boomed. I jumped. Kids shrieked. The boys popped off the palisade like clay pigeons, disappearing from view behind the crowd. Billington sprang from his seat and started down the hill. I ran after him and grabbed his arm, my heart lurching. "They can't be. . . ."

He pointed wordlessly toward the bottom of the hill. The crowd parted to let a chaperone through. He yanked the boys up and ordered the group back to the bus. My knees buckled. I felt giddy with relief. "For a moment there, I thought he'd really shot them," I babbled.

Billington stared stonily past me. "Not this time," he muttered. The Pilgrim with the musket marched up the hill toward us. A short man with the strut of a four-star general, he had to be Plimoth's own Captain Myles Standish.

"Thar's no cause for alarm, mistress—just a spot o' trouble wi' some lads," Standish said when he was abreast of us. Then with a sly look at Billington, he added, "An' if sartain fathers like Goodman Billington har did keep better governance o'er their sons, I wouldna have to use my piece for swich poorpose."

" 'Tis not my sons, but thine own hasty temper that maketh for trouble, Captain Shrimpe," Goodman Billington growled.

"Nay, Goodman, 'twas thine own son John did near destroy our ship with his reckless deed."

A woman emerged from the hovel. She had a round, ruddy face with the weathered look of an apple left on the ground too long. Beryl Richards. Or in her Pilgrim persona, Goodwife Billington. "Beware whom thou speakest ill of, Captain!" she cried.

Drawn by the drama, a new crowd formed. The three Pilgrims traded further insults, then Goodman Billington sliced the air with his knife and vanished into the hovel. "Would we had banished this wild, profane, and troublous man two years afore!" Standish declared to the audience. Turning sharply on his heel, he strode up the hill.

Goodwife Billington shook a fist after him. "Rue I th' day we came to this desolate place to dwell among these dour people an' such a choleric captain as thou!"

Listening to her, I understood why Beryl Richards had cast herself in this role; the shrewish Elinor Billington was a great part for a character actor. A Japanese businessman in a three-button Armani suit obviously agreed with me. He caught the scene with a camcorder perched on his shoulder like a black bird of prey with a red, blinking eye.

Goodwife Billington turned back to the camera. "We cast our lot with these heretics only because they promised us land. We thought we were going to Virginia to grow tobacco and prosper. Instead they brought us to this poor barren place, where we have toiled for seven years wi'out a plot o' land to call our own. Had we but known how 'twould fall out, we should never have left London. For my husband did good business there as a fripperer." Merriment flickered in Goodwife Billington's brown eyes despite her stern expression. Her gaze met mine, inviting complicity.

I took my cue. "What's a fripperer?"

"One who trades in clothes that others—fine folk,

mind ye—have worn." Goodwife Billington glanced quickly up and down the street, then stage-whispered, "Lest some har tell thee otherwise, ye have it from me that hardly ever did he steal th' clothes o' corpses. Now I must take my leave. My husband will be wantin' his dinner."

In other words, show's over, folks.

Goodwife Billington disappeared into the hovel. The crowd broke up. The Japanese businessman trained his red-eyed bird elsewhere. I wondered what he thought of this live-action American history. Next to Nintendo, it was pretty tame. I looked at my watch. Fifteen minutes to go. I considered following Goodwife Billington into the hovel, but decided against it, not wanting to ask her about Caroline in front of her hangdog husband. Besides, maybe I could persuade Caroline to break early.

I poked my head into the Allerton house. Raw meat remained on the table, but the sausage-maker was gone. Spider legs of unease crept up the back of my neck. Relax, I told myself, she's probably stepped out for a few minutes. I made a hasty check of the garden and several of the neighboring houses without finding Caroline. She had said noon, hadn't she? I trotted toward the gate the interpreters used for their comings and goings. Just outside the palisade, a Pilgrim stood with his ax poised over a pile of wood.

"Have you seen Car—Mistress Allerton?"

Lowering the ax, the Pilgrim regarded me speculatively. He was craggily handsome with a curly russet beard. One eye matched his hair; the other was a disconcerting mix of brown and blue.

"Mistress Allerton be gone ta her husband i'—"

"When?" I cut in.

He tugged at his beard. "A farthin' o' an hour ago, methinks."

"But she told me she was taking her break at noon. We were supposed to meet then. I can't believe she'd just up and leave. What's going on?" My voice rose with my anxiety.

The Pilgrim's face went blank.

I glanced around. No one was in sight. "Talk to me. Please. I'm Caroline's aunt. I need to know where she is." I clutched at his sleeve in my eagerness.

The Pilgrim's expression darkened, the blue in one eye becoming the gray of old ice. He plucked my hand away. "I canna help thee."

I stared at him, stunned by the rebuff. He turned away, raised the ax and swung. The blade hit the wood with a loud crack. A chunk bounced off like a head from an executioner's block.

2

"This morning good-wife Allerton was delivered of a son, but dead born." *Mourt's Relation*

I hung around Plimoth Plantation for over an hour. When Caroline didn't return, I cruised the streets around the village and downtown Plymouth, hoping to catch sight of her. I even checked several restaurants, finally choosing one for a solitary meal. By the time I finished it was nearly 3:00 P.M. Puzzled and annoyed, I drove to Caroline's twentieth-century home to wait.

Caroline lived in a playhouse that had been converted into an apartment after her landlord and landlady's children had grown up and scattered. Skirting the main house, I crossed a stretch of lawn, found the key under a pot of frost-blasted mums, and let myself in.

With its loft bed, galley kitchen, and combination living/dining room, the playhouse provided a compact, if cramped abode. It was an appropriate dwelling for someone like Caroline who clung to childhood with a vengeance. The room was filled with kid stuff. The furry red figure of Elmo sprawled in the canvas butterfly chair. Beanie Babies paraded across the futon couch. Coloring books cluttered the coffee table. Disney videos rose in block towers from the top of the TV, one protruding like a black tongue from the VCR.

Whatever was bothering Caroline had to be worse

than a few lost Legos. I prowled the playhouse, seeking clues. The room told me nothing I didn't know already. There were dirty dishes in the sink, crumbs and bits of congealed food on the kitchen counter, soiled towels and a toothpaste-speckled mirror in the bathroom, and a camel's hump of clothes on a chair by the front door. Clearly Mama hadn't been around lately and housekeeping wasn't high on Caroline's list of priorities. To her credit, though, William Bradford's *Of Plymouth Plantation* and other books relating to her work at the village looked well-thumbed.

Abandoning the search, I settled down with my own work. I'd brought along my laptop and a stack of reference books just in case. Let's see. When I'd left Ferdinand Magellan, he'd been about to. . . .

Wham! My chin snapped up from the computer screen. Across the room, a window pane shuddered but didn't break. Caroline? I hurried to the window in time to glimpse a shadowy figure in a hooded sweatshirt disappearing around the side of the main house. Not your usual mail carrier or delivery person. Who then? And what had he left behind?

I hurried outside. Running footsteps sounded on the sidewalk. A car door slammed. An engine revved. He'd be gone by the time I reached the street. I scanned the darkening yard for the missile. The patchy brown lawn was empty except for a birdbath tilted at an angle on the uneven ground.

A flash of color caught my eye. A chartreuse tennis ball lay on the ground below the window, half-hidden behind the pot of mums. A piece of paper was rubber-banded to the ball. I slid off the rubber band and unfolded the paper. In the waning light the Gothic script, cut and pasted from a newspaper, resembled gnarled trees, spiky plants, and fantastic creatures clawing at one another.

I went back inside. The weird plants and animals became words: "Beware th' drowned man whom it pleased th' Lord to raise from his wat'ry bier."

What on earth? For the second time today a sentence had me stumped. First "Myles Standish Is a Murderer," now this bizarre warning. Who was the drowned man? A Pilgrim? But which one? And why be wary of him?

This could be nothing more than a joke. But Caroline *had* sounded upset last night, *had* vanished mysteriously from the village this afternoon. What if she were in real danger? Even worse, what if the warning had come too late?

Whoa! I was starting to think like Caroline's mother, who imagined deadly microbes on every surface, muggers behind every tree. But where to draw the line between paranoia and legitimate worry?

I reattached the note to the ball and put it on the coffee table. It was a few minutes after five. I'd give Caroline another fifteen minutes before putting out an all-points bulletin.

When Caroline burst through the door at five-forty-nine, she'd used up two extra grace periods and I was fast approaching a frenzy worthy of her mother. She greeted me with a guilty rush of words and motion. She dropped her pocketbook on the floor, tore off her coat and beret, and flung them onto the "clothes" chair. Then she began peeling off her Pilgrim costume, chattering like a squirrel on speed. I listened with a mixture of relief and rising annoyance.

"Omigod, Miranda, have you been here all this time? I'm awfully sorry about this afternoon. Something came up. I had to leave early. Looked for you when I got back, but you'd already gone. I thought you'd driven back to Cambridge."

"I waited at the village for more than an hour," I said testily.

"I *am* sorry, Miranda."

She looked at me, big-eyed and beseeching, and as always I relented. "Okay, but why did you burst into tears and hang up on me last night?"

"You caught me at a bad time. I'd just gotten off the phone with Mom. I was worn out, my period had started, and I'm sick and tired of having her ask what's wrong when I've barely opened my mouth. I let her have it. Then you called and I lost it again."

The speech sounded plausible but well-rehearsed. "That's all?"

"Ye-s-s." Lowering her gaze, Caroline fumbled with the laces of the whalebone corset all female interpreters were required to wear. "I'm sorry you came here for nothing. I know how busy you are."

"It's all right. Really." I waited a beat, then said, "Since we couldn't do lunch, why don't I take you out for a lobster dinner?" After eating a healthy portion of her favorite crustacean she'd be more forthcoming, I figured.

Caroline's face lit up at the mention of lobster. "I'd love that but—" She bit her lip. "I'd better take a rain check. There's a party tonight and I need to shower, change, and get myself over to Cohasset." Pulling out hairpins and popping them into her mouth, she hurried past me to the bathroom.

She wasn't getting off that easily. I picked up the tennis ball from the table and followed her.

Caroline stood before the mirror, brush in hand, face hidden by her waist-length mane.

"You got a message," I said.

The brush stopped in midstroke. "Voice or e-mail?"

"Neither."

Caroline flung her hair back from her face. I tossed her the ball. She caught it with cupped hands. "What's this?"

"You tell me. Someone slammed it into the window about an hour ago."

Frowning, Caroline removed the note from the ball and read. An angry flush spread from her neck into her face. Her lips parted, but the only sounds were the plop of the tennis ball on the floor and the crackle of paper in her shaking hands. Her color paled from red to white. She looked the personification of her Pilgrim name: Fear.

3

"And though he was something ill with it, yet he lived many years after...." Of Plymouth Plantation

"That's it?" I squinted through the rain-splattered, wiper-slashed windshield. Caroline nodded.

The dark-shingled house hulked on a cliff overlooking the ocean at Cohasset. Turreted with brooding, eye-browed windows, it was a mansion worthy of a Newport nabob. Or a drowned man? Not likely. Our host and hostess were Seth Lowe, a.k.a William Bradford, and his wife, Nan. I didn't recall any story of William Bradford's drowning and subsequent resurrection. Still, the mystery man might be among the guests.

I didn't usually crash parties, but I couldn't let Caroline go to this one alone. Not when she seemed so obviously frightened of someone other than the Lord. After her initial reaction, she'd dismissed the warning as a stupid joke, refusing to speculate about the identity of the drowned man or the messenger. Something was going on and I intended to find out what.

I parked along a circular drive that led to the house. Then we made a run for it, huddled under a Winnie the Pooh umbrella. At the entrance, a maid with the accented lilt of the West Indies took our coats and umbrella and pointed us down a long hallway decorated with an Oriental runner.

Candles flickered in sconces, casting weird shadows on the walls. The hallway opened into a large formal living room set off by an exquisitely carved archway.

The room was ablaze with lights and already filled with guests, their voices booming as if they were wearing body mikes. Caroline and I descended three steps from the hall into the living room. Almost immediately, a woman with classic features framed by a blonde pageboy swept over to us. Her flared green-and-black plaid taffeta skirt and white silk blouse with lace jabot were straight from Talbot's, her glittering smile straight from the society pages.

"Caroline, darling, so glad you could come!" She draped an arm around my niece and squeezed tight. Then she turned to me. Her steely gaze took in the wrinkled flowered rayon dress retrieved from the bottom of Caroline's "clothes" chair and the clunky black shoes, also borrowed, that made me feel as if I'd sprouted hooves. If I made any fashion statement at all it was "put-together-at-the-last-minute."

"Nan, this is my aunt, Miranda Lewis," Caroline said.

"Fabulous! I've been dying to meet you. Caroline's told me so much about you." Nan Lowe promptly turned her back on us to welcome a distinguished-looking man with silver hair.

"Lyle Eldridge. He's on the board," Caroline whispered. Her gaze ricocheted around the room, seeking someone. The person who'd sent the warning? Or the drowned man?

I stamped an anxious hoof. "Let's get drinks."

Armed with chardonnay for me and designer water with a twist for Caroline, we joined a small group by the bar. Beryl Richards was talking with the hangdog Pilgrim from the village, and an anorexic young woman in a black mini skirt with a bloodless face and a crimson gash for a mouth. The rouge-and-noir motif was repeated in her hair where red plastic clips created dark tufts like bat's wings. Beryl Richards introduced her as Nikki Taverna, the hangdog Pilgrim as Harvey Basile.

"As in chili," he chimed in. "In my other life I'm the

infamous John Billington."

"The only Pilgrim to be hanged!" Nikki Taverna crowed.

The hanged man, not the drowned man. I could scratch him from the list of possibilities.

Crooking a skinny arm around his neck, Nikki Taverna pretended to strangle him. His eyes bulged, his tongue lolled, and he made choking noises. What a couple of clowns. They weren't feeling any pain. Caroline, on the other hand, was all nerves. Rattling the ice in her glass, she continued to glance worriedly around. Basile rubbed his neck and muttered something that was lost in the rattle of Caroline's ice cubes. "What?" I resisted the urge to take the glass from her hand.

"Said I was ready to hang myself before I became a Pilgrim," he repeated.

"Oh really?" I remarked with mock surprise, though this wasn't hard to imagine. He had the mournful eyes of a basset hound and jowls worthy of Richard Nixon. I wondered if aging or some great sorrow had caused the downward drift of his face.

"Harve used to sell insurance, see," Nikki Taverna explained. "Spent the day on the phone being Mr. Nice Guy when all he wanted to do was tell those people to go to hell."

"And now that he's John Billington he can do it," Beryl Richards said. Offstage, she still spoke with an accent—the rich consonant-rolling tones of her native Wales. She turned to me with a twinkle in her eye. "As you may have gathered, Billington didn't belong to the Separatist congregation. He was one of the so-called Strangers in the *Mayflower* company. Bradford described the Billingtons as 'one of the profanest families amongst them.' The Billingtons frequently clashed with the Pilgrim leaders. You witnessed one of those clashes today when he and Captain Standish—"

"Where is Ray, anyway?" Caroline interrupted.

Nikki Taverna fiddled with a plastic hair clip. "He was supposed to pick me up, but then he phoned to say he was running late and I should go on without him."

"He's got something planned for tonight," Basile said.

Caroline's glass shook so violently that water sloshed out. "What?"

Basile shrugged. "Show n' tell, kiss n' tell." He laughed mirthlessly. "Knowing Ray, it could be anything."

Caroline's eyes widened with alarm. Then, without another word, she bolted.

"What's with her?" Nikki Taverna's brow puckered. What indeed? I'd give all my anticipated *ARGG* royalties for the answer to that question.

"The end of the season is always a stressful time," Beryl Richards murmured sympathetically. "Maybe she needs a day off."

I would've liked to get Beryl's take on the warning but didn't want to mention it in front of the others. Excusing myself, I went after Caroline. I found her huddled in a far corner of the room with the Pilgrim with the disconcerting dual-colored eye. With her pre-Raphaelite prettiness and his craggy good looks they made an attractive, if argumentative, pair. While she mouthed an impassioned appeal, he frowned and shook his head. I edged closer, straining to catch their words.

"I only want to. . . ." She leaned toward him, so close they were practically touching.

"No! I'll handle it." He backed away and bumped into an end table with a Chinese porcelain bowl. The bowl wobbled. He grabbed it. I imagined him bringing the bowl down on Caroline's head the way he'd brought the ax down on the wood. The bowl steadied, he removed his hand.

"Robert Redford or Ralph Fiennes?" A chubby young man with a cherubic face framed by dark curls asked at my elbow.

"Huh?"

"Saw you staring at Conor and wondered who he reminded you of."

"Neither actor, though. . . ." I studied him, aware of a faint glimmer of recognition. "He does look familiar. Who is he?"

"Conor Day," the cherub replied. "You've probably seen him at the village. He plays Master John Howland."

"Yes, but I could swear I've seen him elsewhere."

"Could be. Conor's a real actor. One of the few of us who is."

"You're an interpreter?"

"Goodman Annable, a.k.a Zack Shaw."

"Miranda Lewis, Caroline's aunt."

"No kidding. Maybe you could. . . ." He gazed at me hopefully, then his expression changed and he looked more like a fallen angel than one of the heavenly host. "Never mind."

I glanced back toward Caroline and Conor Day, but they were gone. She'd pulled another disappearing act. And this time with someone who made me distinctly uneasy. For all I knew he was the drowned man.

"Think I need a refill," I told Zack and darted off to look for them. They were nowhere in the living room. I hurried up the steps into the hall. On my left, French doors opened onto well-landscaped grounds. I peered out. The rain had stopped, but I saw no one. At the far end of the hall was a closed door. I tried the knob. "Just a minute!" a woman called. The downstairs bathroom.

On my right was another door, also shut. Muffled voices sounded within. Caroline and Conor? I pressed my ear to the door.

"He's got to be stopped," a man declared angrily. "Firing his musket around schoolchildren! Think of the lawsuits if someone had been hurt. Then he has it out with a demonstrator. So far we've managed to keep it peaceful, but a few more incidents like today's and this thing could blow up in our faces. Picture the headlines: 'Pilgrims and Indians Battle at Plimoth Plantation.' We don't need that kind of publicity. Not with Thanksgiving less than a week away."

"I'll speak to him," another man said.

". . . hell to pay if you don't."

The door swung open. I hopped backward in time to avoid board member Lyle Eldridge, now livid-faced. Without so much as a glance at me, he strode down the hall. William Bradford—or rather Seth Lowe—emerged from the room, visibly shaken by his time on the carpet. He started to walk past me, then as an afterthought inquired, "Weren't you at the village today?"

I nodded and introduced myself as Caroline's aunt.

"Yes, now I remember. You're an historian. You live in Cambridge and teach at Harvard." He regarded me with interest.

"Correct on the first two counts but not the last. My ex-husband was an assistant professor at Harvard. I write American history texts for children."

Disappointment flickered in Lowe's eyes, but he recovered instantly. "Wonderful. It's so important to get children interested early on. I have an entire library devoted to American history in there. Would you like to take a look?"

I smiled, sensing a kindred spirit. "Thanks. I would but another time." I was about to excuse myself when it occurred to me to ask, "Is there a Pilgrim who could be described as 'the drowned man whom it pleas'd th' Lord to raise from his wat'ry bier'?"

Lowe frowned and tugged at his shock of graying hair. "It sounds like—"

"Seth!" Nan Lowe stood at the end of the hall, her society-page simper replaced by a scowl.

Lowe looked at me apologetically. "I'd better get back to the party."

Returning myself, I spotted Caroline and Conor Day seated at the opposite end of the living room, balancing plates of food on their laps. They had obviously helped themselves from a buffet table set up in another room. And I thought he'd spirited her away. Get a grip, Miranda, I scolded myself.

But hold on. Caroline's face turned red, her fingers clawed at her throat. Was she choking? Before I could get to her and perform a quick Heimlich maneuver, Conor Day patted her on the back. She gulped water, smiled sheepishly. Another false alarm. But I'd feel better by her side. I took a step forward, mentally calculating the number of toes I'd have to avoid treading on to reach her.

"Plenty of room right here."

A short man smirked at me from a church pew in the hallway. With his gleaming black Grecian Formula hair, dark slacks, and matching sport coat of some faintly shiny fabric, he resembled an oil-slicked seal. I recognized him as

Myles Standish. The man who'd shot off his gun while at the village and who had something planned for tonight, the very mention of which had sent Caroline scurrying off like a scared rabbit. Was he the person she'd been warned against? I glanced back at her. She and Conor Day were eating and chatting companionably. It was probably okay to leave her awhile longer. I sat down beside Standish.

"Smart gal."

Gal? Twenty years ago, when I was fresh into feminism, the word would've made me wince. Now it had a quaint, old-fashioned ring, transporting me back to simpler times when men were men and women were gals or girls. I smiled indulgently.

"Ray McCarthy, formerly of Boston PD, now commander-in-chief of the New Plimoth militia," he introduced himself.

"You were a cop?"

"In another life." He eyed me appraisingly. "But let's talk about you. Bet I can guess. You're a friend of Nan's and still shell-shocked 'cuz it's only been a few weeks since your hubby of nineteen years ran off with a forklift operator."

Shaking my head with equal parts annoyance and amusement, I stole a glance at Caroline. She was looking straight at me; from her horrified expression you'd have thought I was sharing a seat with a serial killer instead of a harmless busybody. I gazed at her questioningly, but she went into a worried huddle with Conor Day.

"Maybe I don't have all the details right," McCarthy continued. "Maybe the marriage only lasted sixteen years. Maybe Big Daddy ran off with a masseuse. Here's more!" He leaned close, splattering me with saliva in his eagerness. "You didn't want to come to this party, but your teenage daughter couldn't stand you moping around the house any longer so she lent you some clothes, shoved you out the door and—"

"Enough!" I burst out laughing.

"Ray giving you a hard time?"

Conor Day stood before us. Up close he appeared older. From the tracery of lines around his eyes and mouth and the sprinkling of gray in his beard, I judged him closer to my age than Caroline's. "Not really. But I do need to have a word with my niece—Caroline," I added for McCarthy's benefit.

He nodded knowingly. "Didn't I tell you there was a teenager involved?"

I scanned the room without seeing her. Not again. "Now where's she disappeared to?" I asked Conor Day.

"Women's room," he replied tersely.

I started down the hall. Conor trailed after me. At the French doors I stopped and faced him. "You know you look kind of familiar."

"Sure. We met at the village today. I was the Pilgrim chopping wood."

"I meant before then. I hear you're a professional actor. Could I have seen you in something?"

His body tensed; a guarded look came into his eyes. Most actors would be flattered by the recognition. This one behaved as if I'd picked him out of a police lineup. "Not likely. I never made it big-time. I've mostly done stock in out-of-the-way places and a few commercials that didn't—" He broke off, staring past me.

Ray McCarthy had risen from the church pew and stood watching us with his hands on his hips. He shook his head slowly. "You'll do fine, sweetheart," he called to me. "But watch out for the drowned man there."

So Conor was the one Caroline had been warned against. Either she didn't know this, or had decided to ignore the warning.

A look of pure hatred passed between the two men. Then Conor seized me firmly by the elbow and propelled me out the French doors onto a flagstone patio. I shook free of his grasp. "What's going on?"

Without answering, he snagged an ivy vine from an urn on the patio and strode up a path that led across a well-tended lawn to the ocean, stripping leaves from the vine as he went.

"What's this business about a drowned man?" I trotted after him, missed a stepping stone, and sank into the sodden turf. Ice water seeped into my clunky shoe, sending a sharp chill up my leg into my spine. Shoulders hunched, arms wrapped tightly around me, I sloshed on.

Conor marched to the edge of the cliff. I stopped several feet behind him, careful to keep a safe distance from the edge. Any closer and my legs would turn to Jell-O. "Why did McCarthy call you a drowned man?"

Conor tore off the last ivy leaf and sent the bare vine spiraling toward the dark chop below. I watched its dizzying descent, rubbing my goose-bumped arms. Conor turned back to me. "Listen an' I wull tell you a dark tale o' a misfortune that befell me, Master John Howland, whilst sailin' thither o' th' *Mayflower* to this brave new world."

"Huh?" The sudden shift to a Pilgrim persona jolted me.

" 'Twas on a stormy night like this whan th' winds blew fierce an' th' seas ran so high we couldna bear a knot o' sail, but must needs drift, I did venture 'pon deck."

With his back to the ocean, standing only inches away from the cliff's edge, he spread his legs apart and swayed as if struggling to keep his balance on a heaving ship's deck. My own legs wobbled. I felt queasy. "Be careful!" I cried.

The words were barely out of my mouth when he pitched backward with a shout. "An' wi' one great roll I was cast into the sea."

"No!" My arm shot out, fingertips grazing his. For an awful instant I thought I'd lost him. Then his hand gripped mine.

"But by God's good providence I caught hold o' th' topsail halyards that did hang o'erboard and runneth out at length." Leaning away from me, he swung his free arm in a circle, miming the unwinding of the rope. My arm muscles stretched to the breaking point; the hand grasping his was a tight wad of pain. I dug my heels into the damp earth and clung to him, terrified that if I let go, he'd be catapulted into the abyss.

"An' lo' tho' I descended sundry fathoms, I kept hold o' th' rope, which th' seamen hauled to the surface an' then by boat hook brought me aboard." He held me at arm's length, then like a demonic tango dancer he yanked me close. We teetered on the brink. Over his shoulder, I glimpsed the dark, roiling water. I shut my eyes. The pounding of my heart and the pounding of the surf racketed into a deafening roar.

Then it was over. I was lifted and set down again. Opening my eyes, I saw we were no longer at the edge. "An' so was my life saved. Tho' a bit o' th' sea stayed in me ever after." He pointed at the blue half of his eye.

I stared into its icy depths, stunned. Shock gave way to anger. "You could've killed us!"

Behind his eyes I caught a quick movement as of a small animal darting across a dark street. "Sorry. Don't know what came over me."

A door slammed. A figure streaked across the lawn, skidding to a stop a few feet short of us. "He's going to do it now!" Caroline blurted out between gasps of air.

"Who? What?" I demanded.

Caroline stared wild-eyed at Conor. He blanched at the news, turning so pale that for a moment I imagined he really was a drowned man dragged from the sea. "He wouldn't dare."

". . . easy as pie." McCarthy's voice wafted down the hallway toward us. He occupied center stage—the top of the stairs leading into the living room. Below him, the other guests were gathered, some seated, some standing.

"What's up, Ray?" Conor demanded.

"Oh, just a little game of Pilgrim trivia that I'm sure you of all people wouldn't want to miss."

Conor glared at McCarthy and took a step toward him. Caroline grabbed Conor's arm.

"Ah-hem!" Lyle Eldridge stood in a far corner of the room, arms folded across his chest, his patrician features stamped with disapproval.

With a nervous glance at Eldridge, Seth Lowe ventured, "Why don't we, uh, get on with the game?" Lowe's hesitant manner told me he hadn't yet given McCarthy the dressing-down he was supposed to. Nevertheless, he was trying to assert a modicum of control.

"As ye wish, guv'ner." McCarthy's tone was faintly contemptuous. "Here's the drill. I give you a few hints about the person I have in mind and you tell me who it is. Nikki will keep score." He motioned for Conor, Caroline, and me to join the others in the living room. They didn't budge. I settled awkwardly onto a step below McCarthy. My arms and legs ached, my foot was numb, and I wanted nothing more than a long soak in a hot tub. But if it was any consolation, nobody else seemed comfortable either. Seth Lowe, standing nearby, jangled keys in a pocket. Across the room, his wife's smile had frozen into a ghastly rictus. Zack Shaw fiddled with something on his finger. Others coughed and fidgeted, jumpy as animals before an electrical storm. The phrase "captive audience" came to mind.

"Ready?" McCarthy asked.

"Ready." Beryl Richards's voice was strong and clear. Only her fingers fluttering at the scarf knotted around her neck betrayed her unease.

McCarthy shut his eyes and pretended to go into a trancelike state as if summoning forth a spirit from the past. An air of hushed expectancy fell over the room. Opening his eyes, McCarthy said, "A pious an' 'umble man, I survived th' terrible cold o' that first winter only to be struck down by—"

"Robert Carver!" Seth Lowe cried.

"Right," McCarthy replied, "but next time wait till I've finished." He started to reel off another descriptive tag. Someone else interrupted with an identification. "Slow down," McCarthy urged, "this isn't a race." But the others went on calling out names willy-nilly like hecklers at a political rally.

"A shipwreck brought me to these shores, me an' my—"

"Fells."

"Meate first for fishes, yet I hope for a glorious—"

"Cushman."

"Pilgrims giveth me th' bum's rush, but 'twas th' Indians who—"

"Oldham."

The words whizzed past, volleys in a game I couldn't begin to follow. Giving up the effort, I focused instead on Caroline and Conor. His gaze was trained on McCarthy with the ferocious intensity of a SWAT sharpshooter. She clutched his arm, again looking the personification of her Pilgrim name. What were they and everyone else so uptight about?

". . . did think to take me by force, but I made fast the doors, armed my—"

"Morton." Conor's voice was barely audible.

McCarthy put a hand to his ear. "What's that?"

"Weston?" Zack Shaw cut in.

"No," McCarthy replied with a glance at Conor. "Morton's correct and that's it. School's out."

The whole room seemed to heave a collective sigh of relief. Conor gave his neck a long, slow, bone-cracking roll. Caroline relaxed her grip on his arm. Seth Lowe's keys went silent. Nan Lowe massaged a jaw that must be sore from the effort of smiling. Beryl Richards's fingers fluttered downward. I still hadn't a clue why they'd all been on edge, but at least the game was finished and we could go home. Uncurling my legs, I rose stiffly and stepped past McCarthy, who was conferring with Nikki, his scorekeeper.

"And the winner is. . . . " McCarthy paused, drawing out the suspense like a presenter at the Academy Awards.

Caroline leaned close to Conor and whispered in his ear. She might have been an actress anxiously expressing a last-minute hope for an Oscar but for the barely audible words: "I could just kill him!"

4

"Now was the Captain returned and received with joy, the head being brought to the fort, and there set up." *Good Newes from New England*

"For the last time, Miranda, go back to Cambridge. Write your chapter. Everything's cool here," Caroline insisted.

Saturday morning and we were still at it, continuing the quarrel begun after last night's party. Only now the venue had shifted from the playhouse to my Peugeot, parked in the staff lot at Plimoth Plantation.

"Then will you promise to keep your distance from Conor Day?" Even to my own ears, my words sounded sternly parental.

"You're as bad as Mom!" Caroline flung off her seat belt. The metal clasp banged against the door.

"I only—"

"Worse!" She snatched her tote bag from the back seat, nearly crowning me. The contents spewed out. She shoveled them back in, jumped out, and booted the door shut.

I watched her plow down the hill toward the Carriage House Crafts Center, which housed the inter-preters' lounge. Halfway down, she caught up with another interpreter wearing a plumed hat, a heavy wool cape, and jeans. He turned toward her and I glimpsed Conor's craggy profile. Dammit!

They spoke briefly, their breath rising in smoky puffs. He looped an arm around her shoulders and they continued down the hill. His cape billowed in the wind, enveloping her like a shroud. The drowned man as the angel of death. Icicles formed in my spine. Caroline and Conor disappeared around a bend. Should I follow?

No. That would only make things worse. By warning Caroline away from him, I'd shoved her deeper into his arms. It was a classic case of reverse psychology. How many times had I done exactly the opposite of what my parents wanted? I'd thought I was asserting my autonomy, but now I realized that my parents' wishes had determined my behavior, albeit in a negative way.

"Just wait till you have children of your own!" My mother's exasperated cry echoed across the years. Childless, I'd missed the heartaches of parenthood but also its joys. For the most part, I'd been content with my role of indulgent aunt, the person to whom Caroline turned for light and air when her parents crowded her too closely. Until now. Overnight I'd joined the camp of interfering adults determined to squash the slightest signs of an independent spirit.

Mentally I replayed the highlights—or rather low points—of last night's argument.

"Conor's the drowned man, the person you're supposed to beware of, so steer clear of him."

"I don't take that warning seriously."

"Maybe you should."

"Why?"

"He nearly killed himself and me with his reenactment of John Howland's fall into the sea last night."

"You're exaggerating. Everybody in the cast gets a little crazy this time of year. Try playing a Pilgrim—immersing yourself in this very different world—from nine to five, five, sometimes six, days a week for eight months and see what it does to you."

"I still say there's something off about him."

"It's not his fault one of his eyes is half-brown and half-blue."

And so it went until, exhausted, we agreed to call it

a night and each swallowed one of Caroline's melatonins.

Now what? Should I go back to Cambridge and hope for the best, or camp out here and try to keep Caroline out of harm's way until her parents arrived? If I stayed and nothing happened, I'd feel foolish, my work would suffer, and my credibility with Caroline would be shot. She'd be convinced I was as controlling as her parents. On the other hand, if I left and she were hurt. . . .

"Aargh!" I let out a howl of frustration. A rap on the windshield told me my car wasn't the soundproof bubble I'd thought. "You okay?" Zack Shaw's cherubic face appeared in the glass.

I gave him a wry smile and nodded. He ambled off, a black plastic garbage bag slung over his shoulder like a burglar's loot sack. He hadn't gone far before he was stopped by Nan Lowe. She wore her version of the grunge look—raccoon coat over a lavender velour pantsuit topped by a long, knotted string of pearls. I wondered what she was doing here so early in the morning. Then I noticed a large packing box tucked under her arm. She'd probably brought something for her husband. The contents interested Zack. He tweaked the twine. Nan jerked the box away and hurried from the parking area.

Zack waited a few moments before he, too, joined the ever-growing stream of interpreters, some in street clothes, others wearing parts of their Pilgrim costumes, moving down the hill to the interpreters' lounge. They carried coffee containers, water bottles, shopping bags, and a hodgepodge of possessions including a boom box, a folding chair, and a quilt and a pillow. What a ragtag bunch of gypsies!

I was one myself. The sprawl of books across the back seat, litter of paper, plastic, and Styrofoam on the floor in front and back attested to my unsettled life since my divorce. Maybe it was time to start cleaning up my act. I found a plastic bag among the mess and stuffed it with debris.

I'd no sooner tossed in the bank envelope than I fished it out again; a telltale bulge indicated there might be cash inside. The envelope didn't come from my bank, Cambridge Trust, but from a local Plymouth bank. It must've fallen from Caroline's tote. I pulled out a bill. Ben Franklin gazed sagely at me. I counted five of him. Five one-hundred-dollar bills. Why would Caroline bring so much cash to the village?

A lurid possibility leaped to mind. My hitherto clean-living niece had gotten involved with drugs and her supplier was here. Unnerving as this possibility was, it could explain her bizarre behavior. She felt guilty about what she was doing and was afraid I would find out. Or, maybe someone was conning her for money, taking advantage of her kind-hearted, generous nature, plus the fact she came from a well-to-do family.

Whatever it was, I intended to find out. I shoved the envelope into my pants pocket and got out of the car. I was barely past the parking area when a hard object whacked the side of my knee. "Ouch!" My leg buckled, but I managed to keep my balance. Tears stung my eyes. The person who'd barged into me swept past in a blur. "Hey!" I yelled furiously.

Midstep, he pivoted. I gaped. Gone was last night's mild-mannered, scholarly host. In his place stood a hollow-eyed man with rumpled clothing, shirttail hanging out, holding a gym bag that had felt as if it were loaded with bricks. His shock of hair stood on end and a fragment of bloody tissue fluttered on his cheek. A nick from his razor or an assailant's sword? He acted as if the Headless Horseman were fast in pursuit. I glanced over my shoulder but saw no one. When I turned around again, Ichabod Crane, or rather Seth Lowe, had vanished.

I rubbed my smarting knee. McCarthy had fired a gun, Conor had nearly catapulted us both over a cliff, and now Seth Lowe had almost broken my leg. Being around these people wasn't safe.

I glanced at my watch. Almost nine. No wonder Lowe had been in a hurry. The village would be open to the public soon. It was probably too late to catch Caroline in the interpreters' lounge. But with luck I could snag a few minutes alone with her at the village before visitors overwhelmed it. I limped back to my car and drove to the main entrance.

Only two demonstrators lolled in front of the Visitor Center, their placards lying on the ground. I didn't see their boss, the big man with the reflector shades. That was a relief. I didn't relish another encounter with him. Still favoring my wounded leg, I approached the demonstrators. The one on my left picked up his sign and waved it lazily. "Yo, Miz Columbus, you're the first comer." His companion sipped coffee from a Styrofoam cup and groused, "With a crowd like this, I shoulda stayed home in bed."

"Relax. Here comes dad and the kids," the demonstrator who'd greeted me said with a chuckle.

"Looks like he's in even worse shape than mom," his companion quipped. The dad held a baby in a Snugli and a toddler in a harness. Or rather the toddler had him in tow. The little boy lunged forward, dragging dad after him.

"I just came to check out the gift shop," the dad confided once we were inside the Visitor Center. His eyes had a dazed, barely awake look, and his hair was uncombed. "*Star Wars, Batman, Men in Black*—kids are exposed to so much violence nowadays." He shook his head. "I want to get them something wholesome for a change. And with Thanksgiving coming up, what could be better than a book about the Pilgrims or some dolls? They'll have stuff like that, won't they?"

I directed him to the shop and went on my way.

A lone Pilgrim tended the charcoal pit outside the stockade. From behind I didn't recognize him as anyone I knew. The village itself looked as deserted as a movie set after a shoot. Only the curl of smoke from several chimneys told me people were about.

I hobbled down the hill to the Allerton house. In the doorway I paused. Caroline stood with her back to me at the rectangular table. She fingered the cloth cover of the wooden basket containing the food she'd prepare for the midday meal. A shaft of light from the doorway illuminated her white coif, a few stray golden hairs, the fair skin of her neck, and the deep crimson of the upper part of her gown. Otherwise, she and the room were in shadow.

When Caroline had first started working at the village, I'd been surprised by the bright colors of her gowns, but she had explained that, contrary to popular belief, the Pilgrims had dressed much like their contemporaries. Now, in her crimson gown, which matched the color of the cloth canopy on the bed behind her, she resembled a Dutch burgher's wife rather than a member of a dour religious sect. In fact, the scene had the exquisite simplicity of a Vermeer painting.

Then someone might as well have slashed the canvas with a knife. Caroline gasped and jerked her hand from the basket cover as if she'd been bitten. She shrank from the table, backing until she crumpled against the wall beside the doorway.

"Caro, what. . . ?"

She twisted toward me, eyes wide with terror, mouth open in a silent scream. She pointed at the basket. I stared at its barely disturbed cover, half expecting a rat to leap out. Nothing happened.

I approached the table cautiously. A few feet away, I made out the sheen of plastic wrap. The basket must contain food after all. I edged closer until I was next to the table. Without touching the basket, I peered in. An eyeball bulged under the plastic. I understood Caroline's shock. They'd given her a pig's head instead of a roast. Seizing the basket handle, I turned back to Caroline. "It's only a. . . ." I glanced down. The cover had flapped open.

The basket clattered to the ground. Ray McCarthy's severed head tumbled out.

5

"... this sudden and unexpected execution ... hath so terrified and amazed them, as in like manner they forsook their houses, running to and fro like men distracted. ..." *Good Newes from New England*

Screams shook the room. Caroline bolted. I tore after her. People popped from houses. A man blocked my path. Hands clamped down hard on my shoulders.

"What the hell's going on?" Basile's eyes blazed into mine.

Bile clogged my throat. I couldn't speak.

"What is it?" Seth Lowe's worried face replaced Basile's.

My words came out at last, coated with the bitter taste of vomit: "In there—McCarthy's head."

Lowe stared at me uncomprehendingly. Then something clicked. Basile had already started for the house. Lowe caught him by the arm. "I'll go." Seconds later, he emerged, ashen-faced.

"Gareth, come back!" the dad with the baby in the Snugli called from the top of the hill. The toddler careened toward us, shrieking with delight.

Lowe whipped a walkie-talkie out of his Pilgrim jacket and tossed it to Basile. "Call security. Have them notify the police and get someone down here immediately."

While Basile made the call, Lowe dropped to his

knees in the middle of the street, opening his arms wide. For a moment I thought he'd slipped back into character, beseeching God for mercy as William Bradford would. Instead he caught the toddler and hoisted him onto his shoulders.

Basile switched off the walkie-talkie. "Security and the police are on their way."

"Good," Lowe answered brusquely. "Keep everybody away from the Allerton house until they get here." Then to the boy on his shoulders he said, "Come, lad, let me take thee back to thy father." He trudged up the hill.

Features twisted into a tragic mask, Basile stationed himself in front of the house. I stumbled after Caroline. A knot of people were gathered in the street below. I pushed through. Caroline clung to Conor, her face scrunched against his chest. Her lips moved, but her words were an unintelligible babble.

Nikki Taverna grabbed my arm. "She says Ray's dead." I nodded grimly. Nikki shut her eyes and moaned.

A siren screamed. Conor shook off Caroline and dove into the crowd. Zack blocked him. They grappled.

"Stop it this minute!" Beryl Richards's voice cut through the confusion. Like schoolboys caught by their teacher in a brawl, Conor and Zack obeyed. "Listen, everyone," Beryl continued, "this is no time for theatrics. Ray McCarthy has been brutally murdered. The police are on their way. They'll want to conduct a thorough search of the village, in case there's . . ." she paused, chose her next words carefully, "more to be found." She didn't say of McCarthy, but I at least heard it. "We will go back to the interpreters' lounge and wait for them there."

"Can I just get my cigarettes?" someone whined.

Beryl shook her head. "No one returns to their house for any reason. Let's get going."

Zack led the procession. I started to fall in behind him, but Caroline remained rooted to the spot. She stared desperately at Conor. He avoided her eyes. I tugged on her arm and she moved woodenly forward. Conor and Beryl brought up the rear. His head was bowed, his face in shadow. He looked like a prisoner en route to execution. Beryl's arm encircled the air around him. The gesture was no doubt meant to keep him in line, but it struck me as protective, too.

Up the hill at the Allerton house, a security guard replaced Basile. He trailed behind us like a stray dog.

6

"We are not any way so much in danger as by corrupt and naughty persons." *Of Plymouth Plantation*

". . . be okay." Repeated aloud in the silent playhouse, the words sounded much less assured than when spoken to the police officer who'd accompanied us here. He was gone now and I was alone with Caroline.

Still in her Pilgrim costume, she lay curled in a fetal position on the loft bed above, sleeping off the tranquilizer a medic had given her at the village. She'd broken down just before her turn to be questioned. The injection had stopped the screaming but made her too woozy to talk. I'd finally persuaded the police to let me bring her here.

I glanced around the room with its clutter of clothes and kid stuff. From his perch on the butterfly chair, Elmo gazed back at me with round button eyes. I blinked. Elmo's glassy stare became McCarthy's—angry and bewildered as if he could neither comprehend nor forgive the awful fate that had overtaken him.

"Be okay." This time it was a command. I shut my eyes and counted slowly to ten. When I opened them again, McCarthy had changed back into the cuddly character from *Sesame Street*. Thank heaven! I couldn't afford to fall apart yet. Not until I'd done the last thing on my mental list.

I went to the phone and dialed. Caroline's mother

answered on the third ring. Before she could ask what was wrong, I told her. I'd anticipated hysterics. Instead Eileen was remarkably calm and in control. Perhaps there was something to be said for always expecting disaster because when it did strike, you were prepared. Eileen said she'd get on the first flight she could, rent a car at the airport, and be here by evening.

I'd barely hung up the phone when there was a knock at the door. Now what?

Peering through the peephole Eileen had insisted on having installed, I glimpsed a face, then the flash of a silver badge. The officer at the door identified himself as Detective Frank Navarro of the Plymouth police. I'd given my statement to another officer at the village but had noticed this man there, too. He was of medium height with a muscular build, dark hair, and the bushiest eyebrows I'd ever seen. Even if he hadn't been a cop, those beetle brows would have made him intimidating.

"May I come in, Ms. Lewis?" His voice was surprisingly mild as if he'd made a conscious decision to compensate for his fierce appearance. As he stepped into the room, he glanced up at the loft.

"She's sound asleep. You won't be able to question her," I said.

"Actually, it's you I'd like to speak with," Detective Navarro replied.

"But I already made a statement."

"I'd like to fill in a few blanks. Mind if I sit down?"

I motioned him to the butterfly chair. My first mistake. Navarro pushed Elmo aside. Elmo giggled and wiggled. Navarro's brows bristled. I winced. "He laughs when you touch him."

"Cute." Navarro put Elmo on the floor and sat down. I settled on the futon couch opposite. Navarro cleared his throat. I sniffed—a nervous habit I'd picked up from my mother. Reaching into my pants pocket for a hankie, I found the usual wad of used tissues but something else as well. The envelope with the five hundred dollars. I'd forgotten all about it. I had no reason to believe the money was connected with McCarthy's murder. But while its purpose remained a mystery,

Navarro needn't know about it. I smoothed my sweatshirt over the bulging pocket, aware of the envelope lodged against my hip bone like a guilty secret.

Navarro didn't notice the gesture. He flipped through a notebook and scanned the pages. "You're the aunt and you live in Cambridge," he said. "Are you close to your niece?"

The question caught me off balance. I hadn't expected anything personal, just facts. The detective's smooth tones reminded me of a counselor Simon and I had seen in a last effort to save our crumbling marriage. And as in that situation I ended up saying things I later regretted. "Yes. She's my only—I mean, she's my brother's only child."

"Seen much of her since she's been here?"

"Not as much as I'd hoped." Unwittingly, the detective had hit a nerve. I'd been overjoyed when I heard Caroline would be working at Plimoth Plantation, envisioning a revival of the very special relationship we'd had when she was a young child. It hadn't happened. "I've been too tied up with my work. But her mother's managed to fly in from California once a month."

"Really?" The eyebrows formed inverted v's.

"Caroline's only eighteen, it's her first time away from home on her own, and if her mother is overly protective, it's because. . . ." I stopped. No need to explain that Eileen had a half-dozen miscarriages before Caroline. Or that arriving well before term, my niece had spent her first months in an intensive care nursery.

"Any particular reason you're here now instead of mom?"

"Her mother was too ill to make it last month."

"What about this month?"

"She and Caroline's father planned to fly in for Thanksgiving and to help Caroline pack for the move back to California. But her mother's on her way now."

"Were you going to join them on turkey day?"

"Yes." I shot Navarro a puzzled look. Why was he so interested in our holiday plans?

Navarro leaned forward in his chair. His brows pointed accusingly at me like the quills of a porcupine.

"Correct me, if I'm wrong, Ms. Lewis. For months you've been too busy to visit. Yet suddenly you take precious time off to come here when you were already planning to see your niece in a few days. Why would you do that unless there was an emergency, unless your niece was in trouble?"

I twisted in my seat, trapped in the web of my own words. "She just seemed a bit out of sorts."

"Did she tell you what was bothering her?"

"Not exactly, but I gather she's been under a lot of pressure lately. This is Plimoth Plantation's busiest time and—"

"She took it out on Ray McCarthy?"

I jumped up, my voice rising with the rest of me. "What're you saying? Surely you don't think Caroline killed him."

Like a trainer urging an animal to return to all fours, Navarro made a downward motion with his hands. "Relax. Several guests at last night's party observed your niece letting McCarthy have it. Do you know why she was mad at him?"

I sat down again. "No, but. . . ." I fell silent. Caroline's verbal assault on McCarthy must've occurred while I was outside with Conor. She'd been all wound up when she ran out to get us. And after the trivia game she'd said she could just— I didn't even dare think the word, lest Navarro read my mind. He was watching me intently, his twin quivers of quills ready to fire. "What if Caroline did have words with McCarthy? She wasn't the only one he rubbed the wrong way."

"Can you be more specific?" His voice had lost its earlier edge, but his brows remained on the alert.

I thought of the snatch of conversation I'd overheard between Seth Lowe and Lyle Eldridge, the look of hatred that had flashed between McCarthy and Conor Day, the tension during the trivia game. The last two seemed too nebulous to pass on. "There was some concern about his behavior at the village yesterday when he fired his gun and—"

"We know about that," Navarro interrupted. "Back to your niece and McCarthy—could they have been having a lovers' quarrel?"

"Caroline and McCarthy!" He might as well have

hurled a poison dart at me. "Whatever makes you think that?"

Navarro glanced up at the loft and made another animal trainer gesture, again reminding me to keep my voice down. "Someone raised the possibility."

"Who?"

Ignoring the question, Navarro said, "So you don't think they were having an affair?"

"No!" I flared, disregarding Navarro's cautionary hand. "She would've told me."

"Would she?" Navarro inquired softly. "Unless there are things you're not telling me, it seems your niece has been less than candid with you."

He had me there. Either I was a liar or an ignorant fool about Caroline. I was so furious it was all I could do to keep from exploding.

Navarro closed his notebook and stood up. "We'll need a full statement from your niece. In the meantime, if you think of anything else, let me know." He tossed a card onto the coffee table. At the door he turned. "One more thing. After the party, you and your niece came back here?"

"Yes. We talked for awhile, then went to bed."

"Sleep soundly, Ms. Lewis?"

"Like a baby."

"And like your niece right now. Amazing what people can sleep through."

I waited until the beetle-browed detective was out the door before slamming my fist into the coffee table. Navarro's card bobbed like a boat in a rough sea. I should've said I'd suffered from insomnia. Then I could have vouched for Caroline's presence at the playhouse all night. Not only had I failed to give her an airtight alibi, but I'd just demonstrated she could have snuck out without waking me. True, the tranquilizer injected into her veins was a lot stronger than the melatonin she'd given me. But Navarro would figure she'd taken more care to be quiet.

At least I'd kept my mouth shut about the five hundred dollars, now scorching the inside of my pocket. And about Caroline's saying she could kill McCarthy. I thought about that statement now.

In New York City, where I'd lived briefly while Simon was doing graduate work, talk of killing someone was as commonplace and innocuous as telling them to have a nice day. People said it all the time without acting on it.

But Caroline was no New Yorker. Rather she was the sheltered product of suburban Southern California with a mom who hovered over her like a helicopter, overseeing every aspect of her life from the food she ate to the friends she hung out with. She'd never had a chance to so much as stumble, let alone fall. Now it looked as if she'd fallen big-time. But into what?

Could she have been involved with McCarthy? My brain recoiled at the notion. He was old enough to be her father, yet very different from her ever-so-proper parent. My big brother Martin was quiet and reserved, McCarthy a boisterous busybody. But she might've been attracted to him for that very reason—he supplied the dash her dad lacked.

A secret affair with a wildly inappropriate person like McCarthy could explain Caroline's breakdown over the phone, her sudden disappearance from the village, and her distress at the party. She'd been terrified I'd find out about the affair and report to her parents.

The phone rang. Conor Day's voice crackled over the line. "I need to speak with Caroline immediately."

"I'd like to talk to her myself, but she's out cold."

"Can't you wake her?"

"What's this about?"

Silence.

"Okay, keep me in the dark," I fumed, "but if it has to do with McCarthy's murder, you'd better tell the police."

Conor's voice grew tight with anger. "Stay out of this, Miranda, I'm warning you."

The line went dead. Now what had I done? For all I knew he'd called from a pay phone around the corner and was on his way here now. I flew to the window and yanked back the curtains. I saw only the back of the main house with its peeling gray paint and the patchy brown lawn with the birdbath tilted like a tombstone in an ancient graveyard.

Minutes passed. Nobody appeared. I left my post and collapsed onto the futon, adrenalin still pumping. I needed to calm down before I could make sense of anything. But I couldn't help wondering about Conor's panic at the village and just now.

I'd call the police. Better to be safe than sorry. I found Navarro's card and started to dial. A knock sounded at the door. The receiver crashed to the floor. Conor? Or Navarro with more questions? My feet dragged with dread as I walked to the door. Behind me, an officious voice announced, "We are sorry, but your call cannot be completed as dialed. Please hang up and try again."

7

"This messenger inquired for Tisquantum ... who not being at home, seemed rather to be glad than sorry, and leaving for him a bundle of new arrows, lapped in a rattlesnake's skin, desired to depart with all expedition." *Good Newes from New England*

"Thank God!" I flung my arms around Zack like a long-lost friend. He stiffened, startled by the unexpected force of my greeting. Then he pressed me close. His body was a wobbly bowl of Jell-O, but his grip was surprisingly strong. I felt engulfed by a powerful mass of protoplasm. Embarrassed, I extricated myself.

Zack blushed. "Sorry. Guess I got carried away. Just stopped by to see how Caroline's doing."

Of course. I'd inadvertently triggered an explosion of pent-up emotion directed at her. Poor guy. As far as I knew, his feelings weren't reciprocated. That must be tough. Though maybe unrequited love was better than none at all, I reflected, thinking of my own empty lovescape. And maybe the strain of that emptiness was starting to tell on me.

When I told him Caroline was asleep, Zack offered to leave, but I urged him to stay awhile. I wanted company in case Conor showed up. From the way Zack's gaze settled reverently on first one, then another object in the playhouse, I guessed he'd never been inside before. He was like a worshiper at a shrine.

"Wow!" he stage-whispered. "I didn't know

Caroline had all this cool stuff. Is that Elmo?" He strolled to where the stuffed creature lay, a red splatter on the floor.

"Don't touch him!" I warned as he bent to pick up Elmo.

"Why? What's the matter?"

"Touch him, he giggles. I can't bear it. Not after what happened this morning. My nerves are shot."

"I understand. Still can't believe it myself. I was a Liz studies major so I know about these things, but—"

"Liz studies?" I queried.

"Short for Elizabethan. Anyway, in those times it was standard practice to decapitate your enemy, quarter his body, and stick his head on a pike."

I held up a restraining hand. "Please!"

"Sorry. But to think that someone would do so in this day and age. And that Caroline should be the one to discover it." Shaking his head, he sank heavily into the butterfly chair.

I perched on the edge of the futon. "And on top of that, the police suspect her."

"You gotta be kidding!" Zack's cheeks quivered with outrage.

"I wish I were, but a police detective was just here. Apparently some people saw Caroline arguing with McCarthy at the party. Do you know anything about that?"

"I did see her speaking with him and she looked pretty mad."

"Hear any of their conversation?"

Zack's curls bobbed as he shook his head. "They were off by themselves and kept their voices down."

Too bad. If he could've told me Caroline and McCarthy had argued over a trifle, she would have looked less suspicious. Still, he might be able to rule out one source of friction between them. Unable to think of a delicate way of putting my next question, I opted for bluntness: "Was McCarthy hitting on Caroline?"

"Caroline and McCarthy!" Zack roared.

Above us, Caroline moaned. Zack stood up with a stricken look. "Now I've done it. I never should've come." He started for the door.

"No, wait." I bounded after him. "I'd like to finish this. Let's go outside." When the door was closed behind us, I said, "So you don't think they were lovers?"

Zack shifted his weight from one foot to the other. "I guess it's not impossible. I've known other unlikely combinations, people you'd think wouldn't get together in a million years, yet the next thing you know, they're choosing a caterer and picking a china pattern. But if Caroline were going to get involved with anyone, I'd have thought it would be—" He twisted the college ring on his pudgy finger.

"Who?" I prodded.

"Conor," he answered miserably. "She's had a thing for him all along. But until recently he's hardly noticed her. Now suddenly they're thick as thieves."

I knew it was just an expression, but the phrase had an ominous ring in light of Conor's panicked call just now. "I noticed that, too," I said, "and it's been bothering me. Especially after she got a warning to beware of him—or rather 'th' drowned man whom it pleas'd the Lord to raise from his wat'ry bier.' "

"I wouldn't put much stock in that," Zack said hastily.

"Why? What do you know about it?" I asked sharply.

"Nothing. I only. . . ." The ring-twisting became more agitated.

"Zack—"

"Okay. I sent the warning. Dumb, I know, but I didn't mean any harm."

"There's no reason to be wary of Conor?"

"Not that I know of."

"You're sure? McCarthy warned me about the drowned man, too."

"He was the one who came up with the line," Zack admitted. "We were sitting in the interpreters' lounge one morning when Conor walked in and Ray said, 'Here comes the drowned man,' etc. I didn't get what he meant at first, but then I realized he was talking about John Howland's being swept overboard and rescued."

"Yes, but could he also have meant something about

Conor himself?" I probed.

"Possibly. Ray did say things at times that made you wonder if there wasn't a hidden meaning. Almost like he was speaking in code."

"What do you think he might've been hinting about Conor?" I asked eagerly.

"I haven't a clue."

"C'mon, Zack, you've worked alongside him for eight months. Surely in that time—"

Zack shook his head again. "Conor's not an easy person to get to know. He talks about books he's read, plays he's been in, but as for personal stuff, forget it. I don't think any of us knows him well. Except maybe Beryl."

Beryl? Why did that surprise me? Because I admired her but had my doubts about him?

"Conor keeps to himself," Zack continued, "and living where he does, it's easy. I'm a people person myself. I'd go bananas without—"

"Where does he live?" I interrupted.

"Out on Gurnet Point. Know it?"

"It's that finger of land in Cape Cod Bay you see from the village."

"Right. The Point's connected to Duxbury Beach, but a bad storm can turn it into an island. Even under normal conditions, it's difficult to reach. Only a four-wheel-drive can make it up the road. Otherwise, you're looking at a long hike up the beach." Zack glanced down at his middle. "Maybe it's not so bad if you're in shape. Still, the Point doesn't attract many year-round residents. But that doesn't seem to bother Conor. 'Course he lives there for free 'cuz he's housesitting. But I'd rather pay rent and live in town."

I thought about Conor and his isolated outpost. Maybe he preferred the solitude. Or maybe there was another reason. Whatever it was, he seemed an odd duck and I didn't like Caroline's association with him. But I found the notion that she and McCarthy had been lovers even more troubling.

"Getting back to Caroline and McCarthy," I said, "I wish I knew what they were arguing about. I wonder if there's a clue in the trivia game. Something about that game really upset her, but it went so fast I missed most of it."

"I have Ray's cheat sheet," Zack volunteered.

"How'd you get it?"

"I asked if I could borrow it. I figured I'd look up the references in Bradford and see if. . . ." He put his ring on another spin cycle.

"You could find anything to use against Conor?" I asked on a hunch.

Zack squirmed uncomfortably. "I'd better be going."

"Not so fast. I won't tell Caroline you sent the warning if you'll check those references in Bradford. There may be something there that explains why Caroline was so angry with McCarthy."

Zack looked doubtful but agreed to try. We said good-bye and I watched him amble across the lawn. Shoulders stooped, head bent, he looked much as he had when he'd left me at the village this morning. Except that then he'd had a black plastic garbage bag slung over his back. Omigod. What had been in that bag? I hadn't thought to ask. Could it have been . . . ?

But Zack wasn't the only one I'd seen carrying something. There'd been Nan Lowe with her packing case, Seth with his gym bag, and a whole host of ragtag gypsy interpreters bearing their belongings in their arms. They paraded past like Halloween trick-or-treaters. Had one been concealing a grisly surprise?

It was too late to go after Zack. Besides, suspecting him was almost as absurd as suspecting Caroline. Just because he was steeped in Elizabethan modes of murder didn't mean he'd used one of them. Also, he had no motive as far as I knew. If he were going to knock off his romantic rival, Conor was a more likely candidate than McCarthy. Unless Zack had been putting on an act when he'd expressed surprise at the notion of Caroline and McCarthy being lovers.

My head spinning, I went back inside. Caroline stirred but didn't wake. I envied her oblivion. She didn't have to struggle to keep the horror at bay. I could use a little help myself. I found milk in the refrigerator and heated some on the stove. Hot milk was an old family remedy. The Pilgrims had believed in its efficacy, too. On an earlier trip to the village, I'd heard Elinor Billington tell a group of schoolchildren that the Pilgrims never drank cold milk—only boiled, which was thought to be a cure for melancholy.

Elinor Billington, a.k.a. Beryl Richards, John Howland, a.k.a. Conor Day, Fear Allerton, a.k.a. Caroline Lewis, Myles Standish, a.k.a.—I had to stop thinking about these people with their dual identities and tangled relationships. I drank the hot milk, stretched out on the futon, and closed my eyes.

When I awoke, the room was dark except for a finger of light pointing across the floor from the galley kitchen where a shadowy figure in a Pilgrim costume rustled about. I spoke Caroline's name. She came over and sat down on the edge of the futon.

"What time is it?" I asked groggily.

"Almost 10:00 P.M."

I pulled myself into a sitting position. "That late?"

" 'Fraid so. I couldn't believe it either when I woke up. The last thing I remember was that medic sticking a needle in my arm. Did he put you out, too?"

"No, I just lay down and fell asleep."

Caroline frowned at her lap. "I want to believe that what happened this morning was a bad dream but—" Her upper lip quivered. "God, it was awful!" She choked back a sob.

I slipped an arm around her shoulders. "I wish you could've been spared the sight. If only you'd left the room in time like your dad used to do."

"Huh?" Caroline stared at me in bewilderment.

"I'd come home from school on days your dad stayed out sick and find him watching some horror flick on the tube. When the really awful part was about to happen, he'd leave the room. But first he'd make me promise to watch and tell him what happened. And dummy that I was, I stayed glued to the set. Giving myself nightmares and doing God only knows what damage to my psyche."

"Dad did that to you? This is the first I've heard. Way he tells it, he was a model brother and you were a total brat."

"Naturally." Caroline and I exchanged looks and the next moment dissolved into laughter. What a relief. We were just two kids yukking it up because horror existed only in the movies, and the only villains were cowardly big brothers. Us against Them. Until I felt obliged to play the heavy. "We need to talk, Caro. A police detective came while you were asleep. He said several people at the party saw you chewing out McCarthy. What was that about?"

Caroline caught a tuft of her strawberry blonde hair and twisted it between her thumb and index finger. "Some stupid thing. I don't remember. Why is this important?"

"Because it makes you a suspect. You quarrel with McCarthy and the next morning his head winds up in your basket. What were you arguing about?"

"None of your business."

"Tell me!"

"No!" Caroline and I had inherited the strong Lewis chin. She thrust hers out defiantly. I did likewise. Chins jutting, we faced each other like beasts about to lock horns. A knock on the door broke our standoff. Caroline hurried to answer it.

Eileen stood in the doorway, crisp and immaculate despite a five-hour flight and hour-long drive. Her short dark hair had a glossy sheen as if just shampooed. Her lipstick, blusher, mascara, and eye shadow all looked freshly applied. Not a knife pleat in the skirt of her lemon yellow suit was out of place. Lemon yellow? No New Englander would dream of wearing that shade in November. Eileen was a splash of Day-Glo in the otherwise drab scene. Her violet eyes flicked from her daughter to me and back again. "Baby!" she cried, holding out her arms.

Caroline squinted at her mother and took a few steps backward as if dazzled by too much brilliance. Then with a sly, sidelong glance at me, she rushed into Eileen's embrace. "Mom!"

8

"... they spent it as vainly in quaffing and drinking, both wine and strong waters in great excess. ..." *Of Plymouth Plantation*

"Such a terrible thing to happen to her," Eileen said in a hushed voice.

And you don't even know the worst of it, I thought. We were standing at the door of her suite at the Plymouth Sheraton. Eileen's worried eyes darted to Caroline, who sat slumped in front of the TV, watching a sitcom. Caroline didn't look up. Having complained bitterly about her mother's overprotectiveness in the past, she was now happy to hide behind it.

"You're sure you don't want to spend the night here?" Eileen asked again.

"I'll be fine at the playhouse. I'll check in with you first thing in the morning. I'd like to be there when Caroline talks to the police."

"Why does she need to talk to them?"

"They took statements from everyone at the village this morning, but Caroline was too upset to talk."

"She may not be up to it tomorrow either." Eileen flicked an invisible speck of lint off the shoulder of her suit jacket, then looked me in the eye. "We don't blame you, Miranda," she said with apparent effort. "And I want you to know that when I told Martin what'd happened, he didn't mention that unfortunate business with the rat. Not—" A blast of laughter from the TV interrupted her. Eileen scowled at the set. "Not once."

Big of him. I said good night to Eileen, then to Caroline, who acknowledged my departure with a curt nod.

In the elevator, I thought about Lotus, the lab mouse that had become the beloved pet of Martin's high-school sweetheart, Pris. When Pris went away to college, she entrusted Lotus to Martin, who was a year behind her. I got Lotus when Martin in turn left home. All went well until I had a big social studies report due and dropped everything else to complete it. When I finally remembered to check Lotus's box in the garage, I found a stiff piece of fur. Martin never forgave me. Over the years he rarely missed an opportunity to point to Lotus's fate as an example of my unreliability. And despite numerous efforts to prove myself otherwise, there were still moments when I not only agreed with his assessment, but felt an overwhelming burden of guilt. Like now.

The elevator doors opened. I headed for the bar. After that last exchange with Eileen I could use a drink. Nikki Taverna sat hunched on a stool at the far end of the counter. This time she was a study in noir sans the rouge— no lipstick and no red plastic clips in her dark hair, which hung lankly around mascara-smudged eyes. She looked at me inquiringly. I explained I'd just left Caroline and her mother.

"How is she?" Nikki asked.

"Not great. What about you?"

"Don't ask." She stared into the greenish depths of her drink.

"What're you having?" I asked after a pause.

"Chartreuse. Made by monks, I'm told. Like to try it?"

I took a sniff and wrinkled my nose. "Smells like mouthwash."

Nikki laughed. "Tastes like it, too."

"Why drink it then?"

"Chartreuse was one of Ray's favorites. Hard to believe that only last night he was sitting right where you are now, drinking Chartreuse."

"You came here after the party?"

"Yeah, for a nightcap. This place was one of our hangouts. Ray liked hotel bars. He liked to watch the people, eavesdrop on their conversations, and speculate about them. 'See that blonde over there,' he'd say, 'she's an ex-nun turned CIA operative.' "

I smiled faintly, remembering the yarn he'd spun about me. I was a people-watcher and eavesdropper myself. Odd to realize I had something in common with the dead man.

"What'll you have?" The bartender stood before me.

"A glass of merlot."

Nikki cocked an eyebrow. "I'd have thought you were strictly a white wine woman."

Read insipid, I thought. "Appearances can be deceiving."

"Ain't that the truth. Take Ray, for instance. When I first met him I thought he was just another guy. Divorced. Down on his luck—I mean who in his right mind would leave a job with the Boston police to play a Pilgrim? But know what? Turns out he's—was this fantastic human being and s-o-o romantic! When I think of some of the things he did." Her eyes glazed over, whether from fond memory, alcohol, or a combination. "And I don't just mean the usual stuff like sending flowers or taking you out to dinner on your birthday. No. One time I happened to mention that *The Wizard of Oz* was my totally favorite movie. That night I came home to find a yellow, glow-in-the-dark runner pointed toward the bedroom where the Wiz himself awaited me."

I suppressed a smile at the image of McCarthy dressed up like the Wizard of Oz. With his short stature, he'd probably resembled Mickey Mouse as the Sorcerer's Apprentice.

"Even bought me this little dog that looked just like Toto. 'Course I had to give him away, because my landlord doesn't allow pets. Still. . . ." Her gaze went glassy again.

I hated to intrude on these happy recollections, but there were things I wanted to know. "Nikki," I began after what I hoped was a decent interval, "some people at the party saw Caroline arguing with Ray. Any idea what it was about?"

Nikki's eyes refocused. "I noticed them going at each other. But I was on the other side of the room. By the time I got there it was all over."

I tried another tack. "Someone told the police McCarthy and Caroline might've been having an affair. What do you think?"

Nikki took a drink and grimaced. "I told them."

I nearly choked on my wine. "Did you actually see them together?"

"Nothing like that." She waved a hand in the air as if shooing away an insect. "But Ray'd been acting funny lately. He seemed preoccupied; he was either late picking me up or canceled dates altogether. I suspected he was seeing another woman on the sly. When I found the art cards I made the connection with Caroline."

"Art cards?"

"Note cards with a painting of a young woman in a hammock. She had blonde hair and looked kind of like Caroline. I thought Ray intended them as a gift for her. When I confronted him, he denied it. But he wouldn't say who the cards were for."

The wine went sour in my mouth. "This doesn't sound good for Caroline."

"Why? Just because they may've had a fling doesn't mean she did him in."

"No, but her arguing with him at the party, then his head landing in her basket suggests to the police she was involved in his murder."

"That's crazy. If Caroline took out Ray, why put his head in her own basket?"

"Exactly. But someone put it there and the question is why. Did the killer have a reason for picking Caroline's basket, or was it just chance?"

Nikki stared gloomily into her now empty glass. "I think we need another round."

After the bartender had brought her drink and my own unnecessary refill, she leaned closer and lowered her voice. "This is in the strictest confidence, understand?"

I nodded.

"Before I came to Plimoth Plantation, I was a performance artist in New York. I did kinky stuff and ran with a rough crowd. Hooked up with a guy who turned out to be a real psycho. Whenever I see a story in the paper 'bout some poor woman getting snuffed out by her boyfriend, I think there but for the grace of God go I."

There but for the grace. . . . The phrase resonated, even though my own recent experience had been very different. Instead of sudden explosions of violence, what I'd known in my long marriage to Simon was the slow erosion of affection through daily nitpicking, nagging, needling. Water dripping on limestone rather than a volcanic eruption. But before Simon, I'd been involved with a man volatile enough to turn on me. I pushed the thought aside. "You think your ex-boyfriend could've killed McCarthy?"

Nikki nodded. "Brent used to swear if I ever took up with another man, he'd kill us both. If he did murder Ray, he put his head in Caroline's basket by mistake. Mine's right next to hers on the shelf." She flicked a lock of hair away from her eyes. "But I haven't said anything to the police yet. If it turns out Brent wasn't involved, I'd rather let sleeping dogs lie."

"How can you find out whether he was?"

"I'm still in touch with people from that time and I'm hoping they can—"

"Thought I'd find you here." Harvey Basile stood behind us, his basset-hound face more mournful than ever.

"Oh hi, Harve," Nikki said, "I was just saying it's hard to believe that only last night the three of us were here at this bar."

"I know." Basile straddled the stool next to mine. "One minute you're alive and the next you're dead. Just like that." He snapped his fingers. "You're driving along the highway and there are these kids with rocks on the overpass. Or you're at a restaurant with your family and in walks this crazy with a semiautomatic."

I gave Nikki a puzzled glance. Her weary look said she'd heard this many times before.

"Or like Ray," Basile continued, "you're having a

drink with friends when all of a sudden the phone rings and it's death on the line. But at least he had the good sense to—"

"Wait a minute," I cut in, my antenna suddenly on the alert, "McCarthy got a call here last night?"

Nikki nodded grimly. Basile went on with his spiel. "Ray was smart enough to take out a policy on his life. He'd been a cop and if anything happened to him, he wanted to be sure his wife and kids would be taken care of. But lots of people lack his foresight. They don't realize there are millions of fatal accidents waiting to happen, millions of potential murderers roaming the streets, lurking in places like this."

"Give it a rest, Harve," Nikki said.

"I don't expect either of you to sign on the dotted line tonight," Basile countered. "But getting life insurance is something to seriously consider. Let me give you my card."

As he whipped the card from his wallet, a small color snapshot skittered to the floor. I reached for it, but he caught my arm, his grip painfully tight. "I'll get that." He retrieved the snapshot and put it back in his wallet. I rubbed my smarting forearm.

"Sorry if I hurt you. I'm not myself tonight. Ray was my buddy. One of the best friends I've ever had. Now he's dead. Murdered. And all because he got on the wrong side of a psycho. I'd like to find that guy and make him suffer!" His voice shook with anger. He scoured the room furiously, basset become bloodhound.

"Take it easy, Harve," Nikki soothed.

Basile's expression softened. Bloodhound turned basset again. His jowls drooped even further as if dragged downward by invisible weights. Then his whole face collapsed like a California hillside hit by a heavy rainstorm. He began to sob, big noisy sounds that racked his large frame. Nikki put an arm around him. "It's okay, Harve, it's okay." She motioned to the bartender, shouting to make herself heard, "A double Scotch, another merlot, and more mouthwash!"

9

"... we heard a great and strange cry.... One of our company ... came running in and cried, 'They are men! Indians! Indians!' and
withal, their arrows came flying amongst us." *Mourt's Relation*

Blam, blam, blam! The carpenters were back. Their hammering inside my head had already awakened me once and
forced an unsteady descent from loft to bathroom. I'd nearly gagged
on the first mouthful of water, but after taking two Tylenol, I'd
forced myself to finish the glass, then a second. Had to start
flushing the alcohol out of my system.

Now, as I flung back the covers and steeled myself for another perilous trip, I wished I'd stopped drinking sooner. Instead I'd
matched Nikki and Basile glass for glass until we'd called it
a night and staggered to our cars. I had a vague memory of
Basile—or was it Nikki?—offering me a ride back to
Caroline's, an offer I'd unwisely refused, though I had gotten home safely. Otherwise, crying and sloppy comforting
were all I remembered.

I edged toward the ladder and extended a leg cautiously into the air. My bare foot gripped, then slipped on
the wooden rung. If I could just make it down in one piece.
I had to reach the bathroom, had to take more pills to dull
the pounding, which grew louder by the second.

At the bottom I rested, forehead pressed into a rung

in the hopes that the external pressure might relieve the internal. It didn't. I stumbled toward the bathroom. The carpenters were outside as well as within. The front door fairly shook with their noise. "Who is it?" I croaked.

"Nate Barnes."

The name meant nothing to me, but at least the banging stopped. I peered warily through the peephole. A blaze of light blinded me. I secured the chain lock and cracked the door enough to glimpse a big man wearing a backward baseball hat and reflector sunglasses. "What do you want?"

"I need to speak to Caroline Lewis. *Now.*"

Clearly this was no condolence call. "She's not here. And you have no business banging on the door."

"Bullshit! I've got every right to find out who set us up."

The door chain danced before my eyes, a feeble defense against his anger. Too bad it wasn't an electrified fence. "What're you talking about?"

"That guy's murder. Somebody's gone to a lot of trouble to pin it on us."

My head throbbed and a wave of nausea passed through me. "You? But who. . . ?" I squinted at him, recognition suddenly dawning. "You're one of the demonstrators."

"Right."

"I still don't understand why you're here."

"The message on the recipe card with that poor bastard's head."

"Message?" I repeated dumbly.

He started to reply, then shook his head with disgust. "This is getting me nowhere fast. I'll be back another time when I can talk to Caroline Lewis." He tromped off.

I shut the door and leaned heavily against it. Thank God he was gone. Now I could concentrate on getting rid of my raging red-wine hangover. And yet what was this business about a recipe card and someone trying to pin McCarthy's decapitation on the demonstrators? His words put another spin on the murder, one that might be worth pursuing for Caroline's sake.

I pulled on my parka over my flannel nightgown. My bare feet scrunched on the wet grass as I tore after him. "Wait. Please!" At his car he turned, keys jiggling impatiently. Across the street a man stopped raking leaves to stare at us. He probably thought we were having a domestic squabble. A scowl from me and he went back to his leaves.

"I'm Caroline's aunt, Miranda Lewis. I come for a visit and the next thing I know there's a man's head in her basket. I'd like to know what's going on myself."

The jiggling stopped. I felt his eyes studying me from behind the mirrored sunglasses. "Okay, you look—"

"Familiar?"

I was about to remind him we'd met briefly two days ago when he said, "No. Like you could use a cup of coffee."

I was mildly miffed he didn't remember me. But then I barely recognized myself in the reflection from his glasses: a puffy-eyed woman whose hair resembled a huge mushroom that had been stomped on.

He jerked his head at the leaf raker. "Get some clothes on and we'll go someplace where we can talk without the whole neighborhood listening in."

The red Jeep Cherokee gleamed like a poison apple from a fairy tale in the midmorning sunshine. It was easy to follow, even for a driver whose Peugeot wasn't known for its speed or dependability and whose own condition was shaky. The Jeep led me to the town pier. I parked and got out, fighting back nausea as the smell of fish assaulted my hangover-sensitized nose. Our destination was a shack at the far end of the pier, Wood's Restaurant and Fish Market.

Nate Barnes and I sat at a side table by a window. "Like something to eat?" He handed me a paper menu with a red lobster on the cover.

I skimmed it. No breakfast items, just seafood and nothing I could imagine getting down except for the oyster crackers. Why couldn't we have gone to a regular coffee shop instead of this stomach-turning fish joint? "Sure," I quipped. "I'll have the clambake for one."

"No kidding?"

Apparently my irony was lost on him. Again I felt his

eyes studying me from behind the glasses, trying to get a fix on me. I shook my head. "A large coffee is really all I want."

"Too bad. Got the best lobster rolls around. That's what I'm having."

While he went to the counter with our order, I gulped air. It was anything but fresh, the smell of fried grease mingling with stale cigarette smoke. He returned with a tray bearing my coffee, his lobster roll, and an order of fries. The coffee was hot and strong. Soon I began to feel its salutary effects on my brain. "Why do the police think a demonstrator might've killed Ray McCarthy?"

"Hey, not so loud," he cautioned.

There were no other patrons. Even the woman behind the counter had disappeared into the kitchen. Still, I repeated my question in a lower voice.

His mouth full of food, Nate Barnes didn't answer right away. A fleck of lobster clung to his upper lip. It moved with his mouth when he spoke, providing a counterpoint to his words. "Because the trail that was left leads to us. There's the demonstrator with the sign calling Myles Standish a murderer. Then a message printed on a recipe card in the basket with the head. 'An eye for an eye, a skull for a skull.' Signed Wituwamot. Know who he was?"

I thought a moment. "The Indian Standish and his men killed and whose head was placed on the battlements?"

"Right. Like we'd want to avenge a three-hundred-year-old murder. We'll get our revenge, but it won't be that way."

He still had his sunglasses on. I couldn't tell if he was joking or serious about revenge. "How then?"

"The casino. We'd rather take your people's money than your lives. This was someone else's idea of revenge."

"Why revenge?"

"You don't decapitate a guy unless you hate his guts."

Who had hated McCarthy that much? Nikki's former boyfriend or. . . ? "Why come banging on my niece's door?"

The lobster fleck jerked into motion again. "She might've seen something. It's not easy to smuggle in a human head and slip it into a basket unnoticed. Also, she knows the bunch over there. She's gotta have a clue who had it in for him."

"You think the killer was an interpreter?"

He frowned at his plate, now empty except for French fries. "Excuse me a minute." He walked over to a table holding various condiments. For a man his size, he moved with surprising grace. Why did I notice that? This wasn't a date but an effort to get information.

"Can't get enough into those thimbles they give you." He dumped catsup from an eight-ounce paper cup onto his plate. "Back to your question. The interpreters have easy access to the village. And they know the historical stuff about Standish and Wituwamot."

"A visitor could've gotten the story from them. I did. And the protestor with the sign about Standish obviously knew the story."

"He was part of the setup."

"You mean a plant?"

"Yup. He shows up that one Friday, just long enough to link us to the victim. Then he's gone. Nobody knows who he is or where to look for him." He popped a catsup-coated fry into his mouth, now free of the fleck of lobster flesh. "But we'll find him. Him and his partner. And when we do. . . ." He dragged another fry slowly through the catsup.

My stomach knotted. "What?"

He leaned forward, his broad face uncomfortably close. "Let's just say decapitation will be too good for those guys." His voice was low, filled with menace. I caught my reflection in his sunglasses. I looked sick. Scared, too. I leaned away, my spine pressing into the chair's hard metal back. My head started to ache again. I needed to pee.

"Just kidding," he said lightly. "But I would like to speak with your niece."

Again I wished I could see the eyes behind the mask. What to make of him? Even if he'd only been joking, his anger was real and he could be dangerous. I didn't want him quizzing Caroline. "Give me your number, and she'll be in touch."

"Don't call us, we'll call you, huh?" There was a trace of bitterness in his tone, as if he was used to being put off by white people like me. Still, he scrawled his name and number on a menu and handed it to me. My head was throbbing in earnest now and the urge to pee was so strong it was painful. I stood up. "I have to go."

"Hold on. I remember you now. You were at the village the other day. You're the woman with—"

I made a beeline for the rest room and remained there longer than necessary. After about ten minutes, there was a loud pounding on the door. "Just a minute." I counted slowly to sixty before unlocking the door. A little girl smiled shyly up at me. She wore a tunic covered with jungle animals over black leggings. With her reddish blonde hair and freckled face, she looked a bit like Caroline had at eight years old. She sidled past me into the bathroom.

Caroline. Damn. I'd meant to check in with her and Eileen first thing. It was almost eleven, but maybe I could still catch them at the Sheraton. Luckily, the hotel was within walking distance. On my way out, I stole a glance at the table where Nate Barnes and I had sat. It was occupied by a young couple. "Look," the woman said in a loud voice, finger tapping on the window pane, "you can just see the masts of the *Mayflower* over there." I hadn't noticed, hadn't even thought to look.

A Do Not Disturb sign dangled from the door knob of Caroline and Eileen's room. I knocked anyway.

Eileen appeared in the doorway, a fury in a fuchsia knit dress. "Caroline's resting," she hissed, stepping into the hall and shutting the door behind her. "You said the police just wanted a statement, but the questions that detective with the eyebrows put to her!" Eileen's voice swelled operatically.

Oh no, I thought, here it comes.

"He wanted to know what she and this McCarthy person were arguing about the night before his murder and what the nature of their relationship was. He even seemed to suggest they were—my God, Miranda, what's been going on here?"

"I don't know exactly."

"What do you mean you don't know? Weren't you supposed to look in on her while I was ill?"

"I meant to but—"

"As usual, you were too tied up with your own work."

"I came as soon as I realized Caroline was upset about something. She wouldn't tell me what it was. I hung around, hoping I'd find out. Then what happened, happened," I finished lamely.

"That's it?"

"More or less. What did Caroline tell the police?"

"That she and McCarthy were colleagues and nothing more and that their argument at the party had to do with you."

"Me!" It was my turn to be amazed.

"She said she saw him coming on to you and told him to back off because you'd recently been through a divorce and were feeling vulnerable."

"That's absurd and not what she said to me." Of course, it wasn't what Caroline had told me. She hadn't had time to make up a story then.

"The detective seemed skeptical, too," Eileen said. "He said he might have further questions and told her not to leave the area. This just keeps getting worse. Caroline probably needs a lawyer. Martin should be able to find someone good."

I didn't share Eileen's faith in lawyers. In my opinion, they were often more concerned with getting their clients off than uncovering the truth. "It's not necessary yet. She's hasn't been formally charged with anything. May I speak with her?"

"Absolutely not."

"Just for a few minutes."

"I know what's best for my baby. And if you'd only looked out for her like you promised, none of this would've happened."

There was the blame I'd anticipated all along. No point trying to convince Eileen I couldn't have prevented McCarthy's murder, or kept his head from landing in

Caroline's basket. Because of me a mouse had died, and because of me Caroline had suffered a terrible shock. Curbing my anger, I said, "I'll check in with you later in the day."

I strode back to my car at the town wharf. Instead of getting in, I followed a paved path that fronted the harbor. After the exchanges with Nate Barnes and Eileen, I needed fresh air and exercise to clear my mind. The *Mayflower*, the Greek temple housing Plymouth Rock, a statue of a Pilgrim man—all passed in a blur. What if Nate Barnes were right about the killer being an interpreter? Zack, Nan Lowe, Seth, and countless others paraded past in my mind's eye. They held up their parcels, taunting me with the words, "Guess what's inside? And guess what I'm going to do with it? Someone's in for an awful surprise and that someone is your niece."

The path ended at the Plymouth marina. I crossed the street and wandered into a park with a brook running through it. At the far end a statue of a Pilgrim woman stood on a boulder overlooking a small pool of water. Her bronze form was weathered a bluish green; her head, upper body, and a foot were thrust forward as if she were bracing herself against the wind that rippled her skirts and cloak. In one hand she held a Bible. The inscription at the base of the statue read: "To those intrepid English women whose courage, fortitude and devotion brought a new nation into being."

The lofty language made me smile. It was meant to inspire, but like most patriotic effusions, it told only part of the story. Few of the women who came to America were heroines and not all of them were English. My job as an historian was to sift through the myths, half-truths, and outright lies until I arrived at the truth—or at least a close approximation of it. This involved raising numerous questions and scouring primary sources for answers. Even so, the truth often proved elusive. Especially now.

Who had killed McCarthy and deposited his head in Caroline's basket? And why her basket? Was it a mistake, as Nikki Taverna believed? Or was it intentional?

Nearby two gulls fought over a sodden piece of bread. One finally claimed it and rose into the air. The other flew screeching after it.

If intentional, then the killer must have it in for Caroline as well as McCarthy. But why? What could she have done to provoke such anger?

The statue stared fixedly past me, as unyielding as Caroline herself. But there must be someone who could answer the questions swarming like greedy gulls in my brain.

10

"It pleased the Lord to visit them this year with an infectious fever of which many fell very sick and upward of 20 persons died, men and women, besides children. . . ." *Of Plymouth Plantation*

"Nay, lad, thee must not go in, for there be great sickness within." Goodwife Billington blocked the boy about to duck under the yellow crime-scene tape.

"Yeah, sure," a man in the crowd gathered around the Allerton house said. "Somebody in there got a real bad headache—so bad they had to—"

"I know not whereof thou speakest, master," Goodwife Billington retorted. "Th' illness in this house be smallpox, a disease especially feared by th' Indians. For they be sore afflicted by it, having no bedding nor linen, but only their hard mats to lie upon. An' as the pox breaketh an' mattereth, and runneth one into th'other, their skin doth cleave to these mats. An' when they turn them, a whole side o' flesh will flay off an' they will be all gore blood."

A few people withdrew in revulsion. The rest continued to pester Goodwife Billington with questions and attempts to get a better view of the inside. Catching my eye, she gave me a weary look. I nodded sympathetically. During a momentary lull, I said, "Beggin' your pardon, goodwife, but the sun be high in the sky and perchance. . . ." She stared at me in bewilderment. I pointed helplessly at the sun, then at my belly. Whenever I traveled in a foreign country, I unconsciously aped the speech of the natives, liberally punctuating my words with gestures. But my attempt at Pilgrimese seemed doomed to failure.

William Bradford sprang to the rescue. "Thy sons be causin' trouble by th' brook, goodwife. 'Twere well thou looked to them. I wull keep watch here." He and Goodwife Billington exchanged glances, then places. She headed for the flanker gate. I fell into step with her. Behind us, Bradford elaborated on the horrors of smallpox, ". . . an' being very sore, what with cold an' other distempers, they die like rotten sheep."

Beryl Richards and I followed a path that skirted the fields and led into the woods. "Is that stuff about smallpox true?" I asked.

"Straight from Bradford's history. The Indians did suffer terribly and Fear Allerton died of the disease along with her sister, Patience."

"But I thought—"

"That it didn't happen until several years later? You're right, but we had to think of something and altering the truth a little didn't seem so bad given what we've had to deal with today. Another morning like this and I'm going to wish the village had stayed closed till things quieted down."

"I know you're ready for a rest, but could we talk? It's about Caroline." I told her about my conversation with Detective Navarro, Caroline's quarrel with McCarthy at the party, and the suggestion that it was a lovers' quarrel.

Beryl listened in silence, the lines in her weathered apple face deepening as I spoke. By the time I finished we were at the foot of the outside stairs leading to the interpreters' lounge on the second floor of the Carriage House Crafts Center. "I'll just get my purse," Beryl said. "Then why not come to my house? We can have lunch and talk more about this."

She was gone what seemed like a long time. Wondering at the delay, I climbed the stairs and went inside. On my right was a kitchen where food of the period was prepared. I caught a delicious whiff of bread baking, but the kitchen was empty. Ahead of me, the lounge door was closed and I hesitated before barging in. To the left was a pantry and a cold storage room with a glass door. A motor hummed. This was where they kept perishables like pork roasts and. . . . Stop it! I told myself. I had no reason to think McCarthy's severed head had been stowed in there. My gaze fixed on a set of shelves painted fire-engine red. They were empty now, but I imagined them lined with Pilgrim women's baskets, one of which had held a ghastly surprise. Before my eyes, the red coating liquefied and splattered to the ground.

"What're you doing here?"

My heart leaped into my throat. John Howland, a.k.a Conor Day, carried an ax with the blade laid flat against his shoulder. I hadn't heard him enter. "I was just—"

The lounge door opened. Beryl stared at us without speaking, the friendliness gone from her face. Conor made a move toward me. Beryl frowned and shook her head. "Miranda and I are going to lunch." He barely stepped aside to let us pass.

Like its owner, the small yellow clapboard house was plain and unpretentious. A trellis with climbing roses was the only ornamentation. On it I noticed the deep blush of a late-season bloom. Beryl unlocked the front door and we entered a narrow hallway that ended at a steep carpeted staircase. A calico cat slipped into the hall, scrutinized me briefly, then streaked up the stairs.

"Love's rather shy," Beryl explained, "unlike her brother, Wrestling."

"Love and Wrestling—Pilgrim names?"

"Elder Brewster's sons." Beryl led me into a cramped living/dining area furnished with secondhand pieces that bore the ravages of her cats. Stuffing leaked out of gashes in the armchair cushions; the couch was covered with a blue fur-matted sheet. Yet the room with its clutter of knick-knacks, house plants, stacks of newspapers and magazines had a lived-in quality that made me feel at home. So did the books lining an entire wall and piled to form end tables on either side of the couch. A few more years without the naggings of my neatnik former husband and my own place might look like this. Already the clutter was accumulating at a rate Simon would consider alarming. I wasn't sure if I'd follow Beryl's example and turn to cats for companionship, though.

The back door opened onto a small kitchen garden planted with herbs, a late fall crop of lettuce, and tomato plants in pots. While Beryl picked lettuce leaves and put them in a colander, I leaned in the doorway. "Must be nice to have salad right at your doorstep."

"Yes. I could use more space, but I'm fortunate that for years I've had two gardens—here and at the village."

"You've been at Plimoth a long time?"

With the colander full, Beryl rose. "Since the early seventies."

"Was it much different then?"

"Oh yes, in those days the village resembled a hippie commune. Older visitors came expecting mannequins of their sainted ancestors and instead they got us—a bunch of long-haired young people walking around barefoot in loose-fitting clothing." She chuckled at the memory. "They were shocked. The Pilgrims themselves would've turned in their graves if they saw some of the things we did then. But we felt a kinship with the Pilgrims that's missing now. Like them, we were rebelling against the establishment. Like them, we wanted to create a perfect society." Beryl's brown eyes glowed. She looked suddenly younger.

I'd been something of a rebel myself, so I knew what she was talking about. I felt a pang for the idealism of those days, for my own lost youth. "You mentioned mannequins—that's what they used before interpreters?"

Beryl nodded. "The mannequins were arranged in tableaux of scenes from Pilgrim life. The guides and hostesses explained these tableaux the way museum guides explain paintings. After they got rid of the mannequins, the interpreters still talked about the Pilgrims in the third person. It was awhile before the idea of having them play actual Pilgrims took hold." Smiling, she shook her head. "Even today some people are unhappy about the change. They miss the mannequins."

"I suppose there are advantages to mannequins," I mused aloud. "They don't talk back. And they don't get themselves murdered."

The glow vanished from Beryl's eyes. She looked old and tired again. "No." She plucked a tomato from a plant, plopped it into the colander, and brushed past me into the house.

There was hardly room for two in the alcove kitchen. While Beryl washed the lettuce, I sat in a dinette chair facing her.

"About Caroline," Beryl began.

"Oh!" I gasped as a tiger cat with gray-and-white prison stripes leaped into my lap.

"Just give Wrestling a push if he's a bother."

"No problem," I fibbed, hoping the cat wouldn't stay long. It crouched on my lap, tail flicking sporadically like a windshield wiper on intermittent.

"I did sense something had been troubling her lately," Beryl continued, "and that she wanted to speak to me about it but couldn't bring herself to."

"Do you think she and McCarthy were having an affair?"

Wrestling's tail stuck up like an exclamation point. Beryl stopped washing but left the water running. "Village romances do occur," she replied thoughtfully. "You take a group of people, put them in a time capsule, send them back to the seventeenth century for eight months, and some will become close friends, even lovers. But if Ray and Caroline were romantically involved, they were very discreet. I thought he and Nikki were an item."

"Nikki's the one who thinks they were having an affair because of some art cards she found."

"Art cards?" Beryl looked mystified.

"They showed a painting of a girl in a hammock. Nikki thought the girl resembled Caroline and that McCarthy intended the cards as a gift for her."

Beryl shut off the water. "Nikki could be mistaken. Those cards could have nothing to do with Caroline. I'm awfully fond of Caroline, you know. It's terrible enough that she was the one who found Ray's head without their having been lovers." The sympathy in Beryl's voice was so palpable I felt almost as if she had hugged me. She patted the wet lettuce with a dish towel as she might have patted my shoulder.

"But what were they arguing about Friday night?"

"Ray being Ray, Caroline probably had a good reason for getting angry at him."

"What do you mean?"

Without replying, Beryl picked up the lettuce leaves and arranged them in a bowl.

"He told me he'd been with Boston PD," I volunteered. "From cop to Pilgrim seems an odd career switch."

"People come to us for different reasons," Beryl said slowly. "Some are genuinely interested in history, others are merely marking time. Still others like Ray want to escape from the present into what they perceive as a simpler past." Beryl turned her back to me and rummaged in the refrigerator. "When Ray first came to us, his life was a shambles. He'd left BPD under a cloud."

"What happened?"

Beryl took out a cucumber and peeled it. "I don't remember the details, but it was serious enough to force him to resign. His wife left him shortly afterward, taking their three children with her. He had a hard time finding another job, but eventually he joined a security firm. He started out at the village as a guard. Later he decided he'd like to play a Pilgrim. He was particularly keen on the part of Myles Standish. It seemed like a good match. Standish was a military man with a choleric disposition and Ray was an ex-policeman with a short fuse."

"He had run-ins with other interpreters besides Caroline?"

Beryl frowned at a tomato on the cutting board. "Yes. Ray could be very inquisitive."

I waited for her to elaborate. When she didn't, I said, "I'm a bit that way myself."

"Ah, but in an historian curiosity is a good thing." Beryl pointed the paring knife at me for emphasis. "You delve into the past because you want to find out what really happened and why. And because you hope knowledge of the past will help you better understand the present." The knife quivered in the air. Beryl's lip trembled. "But Ray didn't care about knowledge or understanding. All he cared about was—"

"Ouch!" Wrestling dug his claws into my thigh. I tried to heave him off, but his claws snagged my pants.

Beryl put down the knife, pried the cat loose, and placed him on the ground more gently than I would have. "I'm so sorry. He's sensitive to my moods and when he saw me getting upset, he thought you were responsible. Let's take care of that."

Against my protests, Beryl hustled me upstairs to the bathroom where she insisted on applying antiseptic and a Band-Aid to the scratch. I felt foolish, but also chastened. Beryl had been kind to Caroline and now I was repaying her kindness with snooping of my own.

Over lunch of salad and slices of a delicious home-made bread filled with raisins, currants, and orange peel, I tried to make amends. "This is wonderful bread. Did you use a Pilgrim recipe?"

Beryl smiled and shook her head. "No, Welsh. We call it *bara brith*, which means speckled bread."

"It's delicious."

"Thank you."

"I've never been to Wales, but I've heard the countryside is beautiful. Do you go back from time to time?"

"No." Beryl jabbed her fork into a lettuce leaf so vehemently the tines hit the plate with a clatter. "I never have and I never will."

Below me, Wrestling attacked the rear leg of my chair. The onslaught continued during the remainder of the meal. But Love, ever shy, did not reappear.

"...we came to a tree, where a young sprit was bowed down over a bow, and some acorns strewed underneath. Stephen Hopkins said it had been to catch some deer.... and as [William Bradford] went about, it gave a sudden jerk up, and he was immediately caught by the leg." *Mourt's Relation*

I walked with Beryl as far as the stairs to the interpreters' lounge. William Bradford was on his way down.

"Seth," Beryl called, "when you get back from your break, could you stop by the Allerton house? I need to speak to you."

"I'll try but—"

"It's important," she said in a voice that brooked no further argument.

Lowe nodded. Giving my arm a quick squeeze, Beryl bade me good-bye and hurried up the stairs.

"I owe you an apology for nearly knocking you down yesterday," Lowe surprised me by saying. "Being late always makes me frantic. Still, I should've paid more attention to where I was going. And I should've stopped to see if you were all right."

I made a dismissive gesture with my hands.

"I was abrupt with Caroline, too. But at least I was able to apologize at the time."

Why make nice now? Either Lowe was genuinely ashamed of his behavior, or something else was going on.

And what had he said to Caroline? I made a mental note to ask her.

"I guess you'll be returning to Cambridge," Lowe remarked.

"No. I'm going to stick around until Caroline's father arrives. Her mother's with her, but Caroline's in bad shape. I want to be on hand in case they need me."

"If there's anything Nan or I can do, just let us know." Lowe turned to leave.

"Actually, there is something you could do for me. I'm writing a chapter on the early explorers of the Americas. I'd like to take you up on the offer to look at your library." In fact, I had all the books I needed, but Lowe's apology had aroused my curiosity; I wanted to speak with him further.

Lowe frowned. "When would you like to come?"

"Later today?"

"Impossible."

"Tomorrow then?"

He seemed about to protest. Instead, with a sigh he said, "All right. Come to the house tomorrow at two."

Rubber rumbled on the pavement above. Clad in her Pilgrim waistcoat and skintight black bike shorts, Nikki Taverna roller-bladed down the hill toward us. "I thought I told you not to do that here." Lowe glared at her.

"What's the big deal? Kids ride their bikes around all the time."

"But that's after hours. And they're children, not grown-ups with a job to do. What if someone saw you? We go to such trouble to be authentic and then you shatter the illusion."

"Okay. It won't happen again."

"Better not." Lowe strode angrily up the hill to his car.

Nikki tsk-tsked. "He's in a foul mood today. Looks like Ray's murder has even gotten to him."

"Even?"

Nikki glanced quickly around. Nobody was in sight. Still, she plunked down behind a parked car. I joined her. "There wasn't any love lost between them. Seth used to act like he was William Bradford reincarnated, but Ray smelled a phony. Seth's wife's a blue blood all right, but he's a Brooklyn Jew, whose dad made his millions manufacturing vacuum cleaner bags. Seth was furious when Ray spread the word about his less than exalted origins. Seth even threatened to fire Ray, but he didn't dare."

"No?"

"Much as Seth disliked Ray, he was afraid of him, too. Ray had some kind of hold over him but don't bother asking me what it was. Ray could be very secretive." Nikki stood up. "Gotta go. Down at the village they'll be wondering what became of Mistress Elizabeth Hopkins."

I rose also. "One more thing. Have you checked out the whereabouts of your former boyfriend?"

Again Nikki glanced nervously around. "Called a couple of friends while I was on my break and got the number of the lady he's currently living with. I tried her but got her machine and didn't want to leave a message." She stubbed a blade on the ground and looked at me. "You ask a lot of questions, Miranda. Is it because of Caroline?"

"That and. . . ." What else was driving me? I wasn't sure, but I felt its pull. "I don't know. Maybe it's simply my historian's passion for the truth."

Nikki rolled her eyes. "I don't usually give advice— who's gonna listen to me, anyway—but be careful."

"I will."

"Ciao, then." She glided to the foot of the stairway and clumped awkwardly up.

"No knee pads, no wrist protectors, no helmet," a male voice clucked disapprovingly. "She's asking for trouble."

I turned to face Frank Navarro, my favorite beetle-browed detective. "I didn't know you cared. About any of them. Except as suspects."

"Now, now. I'm only doing my job. And it sure would make that job a helluva lot easier if your niece cooperated with us. Has she told *you* why she had it out with McCarthy Friday night?" His brows went on the alert.

"No, but even if it was a lover's quarrel, you can't seriously believe she'd cut off his head and put it in her own basket."

Navarro shrugged his eyebrows. "People have done weirder things. And if your niece didn't kill him, she could've persuaded someone else to chop off his head. Like Salome with John the Baptist."

I flinched, as an awful scenario took shape in my mind: Upset over her affair with McCarthy, Caroline had confided in Conor, who'd taken her at her word when she said she wanted McCarthy dead.

"Did I say the wrong thing?" Navarro inquired innocently.

"Your problem, detective, is that you've been reading too much—" I broke off for fear of offending him.

Navarro smiled faintly. "Didn't get it from the good book. Saw this painting at a museum."

"Then you've been spending too much time at museums."

"Cops can't be cultured?"

"It's fine, really. But Caroline may not be the only one who got a piece of—" I stopped, horrified at what I'd been about to say.

"She is the only one," Navarro declared emphatically.

"Then you've found the rest of him?"

Navarro nodded. "A jogger discovered the body this morning behind some bushes at Myles Standish State Park."

"Oh." I couldn't think of anything else to say. I hadn't the heart—or the stomach—to continue the conversation.

Navarro smoothed one eyebrow, then the other with his index finger. "Talk to your niece, Ms. Lewis," he said silkily. "Maybe you can make her see how important it is to tell us the truth. Mama, I'm afraid, is no help in that department."

Back at the playhouse, I telephoned the Sheraton. Eileen said Caroline was still resting, but reluctantly agreed to let me join them for an early dinner at the hotel. Then I dutifully switched on my laptop, hoping to banish for the moment my fear that Caroline was in some way responsible for McCarthy's murder. But scenes from the party replayed themselves in my mind: Caroline in a huddle with Conor, the look of hatred that had passed between Conor and

McCarthy, Caroline's anguish during the trivia game culminating in the words: "I could just kill him!" Far from being banished, suspicion grew like a malignant tumor.

At 5:00 P.M. the phone rang. "I looked up the trivia game references in Bradford," Zack said, "and I'm afraid—no, I'd better tell you in person. I can be there in ten minutes."

I waited for him with a mix of curiosity and dread. The ten minutes might as well have been ten hours. But at last Zack arrived with a copy of Bradford's history tucked under his arm. A sheet of yellow legal paper protruded from the volume.

"It's the one about Mr. Fells," he announced glumly.

"Who?"

"An Englishman shipwrecked near Plymouth with a maidservant who—here, see for yourself." He handed me the book. I read:

> This Fells, amongst his other servants, had a maidservant which kept his house and did his household affairs, and by the intimation of some that belonged unto him he was suspected to keep her as his concubine. And both of them were examined thereupon but nothing could be proved, and they stood upon their justification. So with admonition they were dismissed, but afterward it appeared she was with child, so he got a small boat and ran away with her for fear of punishment.

I stopped reading and exchanged glances with Zack. He looked as if he'd just landed in hell. I felt the way he looked.

"Of course, this may not be an allusion to what was going on between Caroline and McCarthy," Zack said slowly. "I mean it was Mr. Fells, not Myles Standish, who kept a concubine."

Caroline, concubine. The nasty rhyme jangled in my brain. And concubine with child, which gave her more cause for distress and lent a chilling credibility to a scenario with McCarthy as seducer, Caroline as victim, and Conor as her avenger.

Caroline, concubine; Caroline, concubine. The buzz became deafening. I barely heard Zack's worried voice. "Miranda?"

Pulling myself together, I said, "You're probably right. This doesn't necessarily have anything to do with Caroline and McCarthy. But until we know for sure, don't mention it to anyone."

"My lips are sealed." He traced a line across his mouth with his index finger and turned to go.

"Zack," I called after him, remembering there was something else I wanted to ask. "You were carrying a plastic garbage bag when I saw you at the village Saturday morning. What was in it?"

"Some parts of my costume I was taking to the wardrobe department for repair," he replied. "Why do you ask?"

I shrugged. "Just curious. After you left me, I saw you talking with Nan Lowe. Does she come to the village often?"

"No. I was surprised to see her myself. She told me she'd brought leftover hors d'oeuvres from the party for the interpreters to nosh on. Apparently Seth was supposed to bring them but he forgot. If you ask me, I think she came to—but no, enough said," he concluded mysteriously.

"What?"

"My lips are sealed," he repeated with another finger swipe across his mouth.

Eileen perched on the edge of her chair. She looked ready to hurl herself at any lurking murderer. But if a killer had ventured into the Sheraton dining room, he would have found slim pickings. At 5:45 P.M. Eileen and Caroline were the only people there.

"I didn't think you'd mind, so I went ahead and ordered for the three of us," Eileen said as I sat down. "We're having one of the specials—scallops over linguine." She signaled to the waiter, who brought our salads. Eileen attacked hers with gusto, but Caroline wrinkled her nose at the balsamic-vinaigrette-coated baby greens.

"Aren't you going to eat that?" Eileen demanded.

Caroline made a face. "Too much vinegar."

"You haven't even tried it."

"I can smell it."

"If I get you one without dressing, will you eat it?"

"I don't want any salad."

"But you've always loved baby greens and these are especially good."

"You're not feeling nauseous, are you?" I asked Caroline.

"No—why should I be?" Caroline stared at me with surprise.

"Why should she?" Eileen echoed.

"I just thought she might've. . . ."

"What?"

"Picked up a stomach bug," I backpedaled.

"Is that it, baby?" Eileen pressed. "If you'd only told me, I'd have ordered differently."

"Will you both stop it!" Caroline cried.

"I only—"

"Mom!"

"All right. Let's change the subject. How was your day, Miranda?" There was a hint of wariness in the too bright gaze Eileen trained on me.

An hour later, I stood on the curb outside the hotel, as unenlightened as ever. After Caroline's outburst, Eileen had steered the conversation away from anything likely to upset her, and I hadn't wanted to confront Caroline with her mother present. But soon I'd have to, unless I could find a way to get Caroline alone. I scuffed a shoe on the curb irritably.

Caroline, concubine. The buzz began again. Concubine and accessory to murder? A gust of wind rippled the flags by the hotel entrance, rustled a pile of leaves in the parking lot, and blew dirt into my face. I twisted my head sideways in time to see a figure dart out of the shadows and scurry through the hotel doors.

12

"It happened that two of their men fell out, as they were in game, (for they ... will play away all, even their skin from their backs, yea their wives' skins also ...) and growing to great heat, the one killed the other." *Good Newes from New England*

At the elevators he stopped to remove the black-knit ski cap, run a hand through his russet curls, and turn down the collar of his pea coat. I remembered when those coats were all the rage. Now they were back in vogue. Caroline was thrilled to get the navy surplus bell bottoms I'd worn in college. But this was no teenager masquerading in the clothes of an earlier generation.

"Conor?"

Startled, he turned to face me.

"If you're on your way up to Caroline, don't bother. She's not well and her mother won't let her have visitors."

"Too bad. I telephoned several times, but her mother put me off. Bit of a dragon lady, isn't she?"

"Eileen does tend toward overprotectiveness. But after what happened you can't blame her."

"I suppose not." He made a move to go.

"I'm worried about her myself. Could we talk?"

He eyed me warily. "I guess. Want to have a drink?"

"No thanks." Last evening's excess had turned me into a teetotaler—at least for tonight. "Let's. . . ." I hesitated, trying to think of a venue where he'd feel at ease and I'd feel safe. In my experience, men were often the most forthcoming when in motion. But I wouldn't let him lead me to the cliff's edge tonight. No. We'd take a stroll to the harbor, which was well lit and filled with tourists.

After cutting through the hotel parking lot and a cluster of small shops, we came out on Water Street. We crossed it and followed the paved path overlooking the harbor that I'd taken earlier in the day. As we passed the town wharf, I saw Wood's was still open and wondered if Nate Barnes had returned for another meal of lobster rolls and catsup-drenched French fries. But there was no red Jeep Cherokee in the parking lot. Just as well, though. . . .

"What's on your mind?" The question jerked me back to my companion, a skulker again with knit cap pulled down almost to his eyes, coat collar hugging his ears, hands pushed into coat pockets.

"Caroline and McCarthy had a fight at the party Friday. Any idea what it was about?"

"Nope. Never even knew she spoke with him."

"My guess is that it happened while you and I were outside."

"So why ask me?"

"You were with her a lot. I thought you'd know if she had a reason to be angry at him."

"Maybe he said something that ticked her off. Ray had a way of getting to people."

"Because he was inquisitive?"

Conor stopped short. "Who told you that?"

"Beryl."

"What else did she say?" he asked with studied casualness.

I shrugged. "Not much. Sure you've no idea what Ray and Caroline quarreled about?"

"Why don't you ask her?"

"She's not telling. Said it wasn't important."

"Well then." He sounded relieved.

"But it *is* important," I persisted. "She's eighteen. A nice kid. Never in trouble before. A man's head winds up in her basket. The police suspect her because she had it out with him and at least one person thinks they were having an affair."

"That's ridiculous!"

"Is it? Nikki believes they were."

"She's a fool."

"Then what in heaven's name was going on between Caroline and McCarthy?"

Conor took a deep breath and let it out slowly. "All right, I'll tell you."

Hoofbeats sounded on the street behind us. A male voice intoned, "And over there you have the *Mayflower II*, an exact replica of the famous ship that brought the Pilgrims to these shores."

Conor waited until the carriage with its cargo of tourists clattered past. He gazed at the *Mayflower*, rising like a ghost ship in the moonlight. Then he said, " 'T all began wi' a wager twixt Captain Standish an' myself over when th' next ship from England should arrive."

Not again, I thought. Conor had an annoying habit of slipping into his Pilgrim schtick when it suited him. But at least tonight we weren't teetering on the brink of a precipice.

"He said one date, I another to th' tune o' five pounds," Conor continued. "An' I hath the misfortune to be mistaken. Whereupon Captain Standish did demand payment straight away. An' when I, having many burdens 'pon me at that time, could not do so, he became most wroth an' divers angry words passed betwixt us. Which words Mistress Fear Allerton did o'erhear, an' kind, generous soul that she be, she did propose to lend me th' sum."

It took me a few moments to make twentieth-century sense of this. "You made a bet with McCarthy you couldn't make good and Caroline offered to lend you the money?"

Conor nodded. "She was upset I wouldn't take it. The argument with Ray was probably about that. She wanted him to lay off me."

"Why didn't you just accept the loan, pay Ray, and be done with it?"

"No!" Conor stopped short again. "This was between Ray and me. I didn't want Caroline involved. If

Ray found out the money came from her, there would have been no end to it."

"What?"

"Nothing." Balled fists bulged in the pockets of his pea coat. "I'm sorry about the mess my bet got Caroline into. But things will get straightened out. The police will realize her quarrel with Ray had nothing to do with his murder."

"It would help if you told them what you've just told me."

"Yeah, I should do that." His tone lacked conviction. "Ready to go back now?" Without waiting for a reply, he started walking back toward the town wharf.

I hurried to catch up with him. "One more question."

Conor heaved another sigh and looked resigned. "Now what?"

"What was the bet really about?"

"Whether the Patriots or the Dolphins would win the game last weekend. Stupid, I know. But Ray was so sure about the Dolphins, I figured I'd show him up."

"And ended up getting shown up yourself to the tune of five hundred dollars?"

"How do you know the bet was for that amount?"

I explained about finding the bank envelope. "Now that Ray's dead, Caroline can redeposit the money, and you don't have to worry about your debt."

The words were no sooner out of my mouth than Conor turned on me in a fury. "Are you suggesting I killed Ray over a bet?"

I was shaking inside, but I managed to keep my voice steady. "That's not what I said." I caught a quick movement behind his eyes; an otter skittered over blue ice.

"Right. I'm being paranoid. Forgive me."

Was it paranoia or the fear that went with genuine guilt? I wondered. Aloud I said, "It's okay. Everybody who ever had a cross word with McCarthy probably feels a bit that way."

Conor nodded and we continued on in silence. At the traffic light ahead, a car idled, window open, radio blaring. Led Zeppelin belted out *Whole Lotta Love*. My head bobbed to the beat. A vision took shape in my mind.

A man-child gyrates to music. His gray tee shirt is stretched tight across his chest, his jeans hang low on slim hips. He's wearing his trademark beret. Sweat glistens on what's visible of his forehead. Heat radiates from his body, enveloping me. I want to reach out and touch him.

When the light changed, the car surged ahead. The music and the vision died away. "Takes you back, doesn't it?" Conor murmured.

I turned to him, face flushed from the vision. "Yeah. Seems like they played that song at every party my freshman year in college."

"Same here."

I looked at him with interest. "Were you at Stanford by any chance?"

"No, why do you ask?" The edge was back in Conor's voice.

"I'm still trying to figure out where I've seen you before."

"Well, it wasn't college."

"Where did you go?"

Conor stiffened, became cagey again. "A rinky-dink school in Michigan. I'm sure you've never heard of it."

"Try me." I wondered at his reluctance. Was he ashamed at not having attended a big-name school, or was something else involved?

After a long pause Conor said, "Saint Etienne."

"Right, I haven't heard of it."

"No reason you would've. It's not a place that gets much publicity except locally. Even in the late sixties and early seventies when campuses like Ann Arbor were making the news with antiwar protests, things stayed quiet at St. Et."

"So you missed all the excitement?"

Conor nodded. "What about you?"

"I was an activist for awhile. But I got turned off by the violence and destruction of property."

"A lot of people felt the way you did," Conor said. "The Weathermen and the people in SDS were a minority."

"True, but the Vietnam War was the defining event of our generation. I wish I'd found a way to protest without resorting to violence." We'd reached the town wharf. This time there was a red Jeep Cherokee in the lot. It didn't necessarily belong to Nate Barnes; plenty of people drove red Jeep Cherokees. Still, I felt an odd tug in that direction.

"Sins of omission," Conor muttered, "can weigh on you almost as much as. . . ."

With an effort I brought my attention back to him. "What?"

"Never mind. Sure you don't want something to eat or drink? You're gnawing on your thumb and staring at that seafood place like you really want to go in."

"Oh." I jerked my thumb out of my mouth with embarrassment.

Conor walked me back to my car and we said good night. I watched him go, his dark-clothed figure blending easily into the shadows. A question rose like a bubble in my brain. Rolling down the window, I called after him, "What about you—you never said what you did during Vietnam? Were you drafted or what?"

He turned, mouthed a word that sounded like Caroline. I shook my head uncomprehendingly and he repeated it. "Canada."

After Conor had gone, I briefly debated returning to Wood's. If Nate Barnes were there, I could find out if he'd made any progress locating the suspicious demonstrator. But he might press for access to Caroline in return. And I wasn't ready to offer that, wasn't sure I was ready for another encounter with him myself. My feelings about him were mixed. Besides, he knew where to find me—along with just about everyone else who had a possible connection to McCarthy's murder.

Back at the playhouse, I marched over to my laptop, determined to finally get some work done. Zack's copy of Bradford lay on the table next to my computer. A yellow sheet poked like an accusing finger from the volume, reminding me of my folly in letting a jealous girlfriend and a suspicious cop lead me astray. Salome and John the Baptist indeed! I yanked the paper from the book and was about to chuck it when I saw it was McCarthy's cheat sheet for the trivia game.

The sheet was probably the last thing McCarthy had written. Should I turn it over to the police as evidence? But of what? Could the motive for his murder lie in these notes, jotted in a crabbed, barely legible hand, after all?

I scanned the sheet with interest. There was a list of twenty items. Each item consisted of a few descriptive words, then a name. Number three had caught Zack's attention: "Shipwreck/[illegible] = concubine. Mr. Fells." I squinted at the illegible word. It looked like "daughter," but that couldn't be right because Fells's servant had been his concubine.

My curiosity even more aroused, I studied the other items. Number six intrigued me: "butt on breech/hatchet dead, poor"—"devil," "dead," or "dad"? The word had been crossed out so I couldn't be sure. The reference was to John Oldham. I looked up Oldham in Bradford and discovered he was a troublemaker whom the Pilgrims expelled from their colony with the seventeenth-century version of the bum's rush—whacks on the seat of his pants from the butts of their muskets. Later, trading with Indians in another part of New England, the unfortunate Oldham had his head bashed in by an Indian hatchet.

Poor McCarthy. When he'd expressed sympathy for Oldham's fate, he'd little dreamed his own head would soon roll.

I looked up the next thirteen references without finding anything remarkable in McCarthy's notes or the stories themselves. The last entry, number twenty, was the shortest: "Armory. Thomas Morton."

Morton was another colorful, if disreputable figure in Pilgrim history. He and his cronies led a life of drinking and dissipation at a settlement called Merrymount. They especially angered the Pilgrims by selling guns to the Indians. Bradford inveighed against this trade at length. When Morton refused to end it, the Pilgrims sent a small army, headed by Myles Standish, against him. Morton and his men holed up in their fort but proved too drunk to defend themselves. The only mishap occurred when one of Morton's inebriated men accidentally sliced his nose on the point of a sword.

Ordinarily, the scene's Falstaffian flavor would have made me smile. Not tonight. I couldn't shake the sense that something in these notes, penned by a man now dead, in the stories themselves, chosen for reasons unknown to me, held the key to McCarthy's murder. The violence in the stories, whether real or merely threatened, seemed to foreshadow McCarthy's own violent end.

I closed the fat volume of Bradford's history with a thud, and sat in silence for a few minutes. Under other circumstances I would've appreciated this quiet, an advantage of the playhouse's set-back-from-the-street location. But after the noise and commotion of the past few days, the silence now was almost eerie. I would've welcomed a knock on the door or a phone call and was half tempted to make one myself, but couldn't think whom to call. So I simply sat there, exhausted but on edge, listening to the silence and trying to hear what lay beyond it.

When I finally did fall asleep, hatchet-wielding Indians and white men with guns stalked my dreams. Waking from one nightmare of being chased by an unknown man with an ax, I was so spooked that I got up and shoved the butterfly chair against the door, barricading myself in the playhouse like Thomas Morton in his fort.

13

"Yet, because love thinks no evil nor is suspicious, they took his fair words for excuse...." *Of Plymouth Plantation*

"Hello, you have reached Zack Shaw's machine. Please don't hang up without leaving a message—any message. Or the answer to this riddle: 'What doth a rich man put i' his pocket an' a poor man—"

"Uh, got it," Zack's sleepy voice broke into the recording.

"It's Miranda. Sorry to wake you, but I wanted to let you know we were wrong about Caroline and McCarthy." I told him the gist of my conversation with Conor.

I'd expected him to be relieved. Instead his voice was laced with bitterness. "She was gonna lend Conor all that money, even went to bat for him with Ray, then took the heat herself because she didn't want it to look bad for pretty boy. What some people will do for—she could be protecting a murderer!"

My grip tightened on the receiver as an image of the killer digitalized in my brain. A man with an ax. "What makes you think that?"

"He's got a motive because he owed Ray money. And he had the opportunity to—"

"Conor doesn't have an alibi?" I broke in excitedly.

"I meant he had the opportunity to slip the head in

her basket when—" He stopped.

"What?" I prodded.

"Forget it. It's jealousy talking. I hate myself when I get this way."

"Zack—"

"No."

"At least tell me the answer to the riddle on your machine." Anything to keep him talking.

"Snot."

"Huh?"

"A rich man wipes the snot from his nose with his handkerchief and puts it into his pocket, while a poor man simply tosses the snot onto the ground."

On that edifying note, Zack said good-bye. I'd promised myself that after this call I'd devote the morning to work, so I switched on my laptop. My resolve lasted all of five minutes. Only a short while ago, I could've happily spent hours hobnobbing with the early explorers of the New World. Now I felt hemmed in by the present, caught in a quagmire of questions about McCarthy's murder and why his head had wound up in Caroline's basket. And with every step I took toward getting answers, I felt myself sinking in deeper.

Jealousy may have prompted Zack's words just now, but they could still be true. He might've observed Conor hanging around the shelves where the baskets were kept, or he could've seen him sneak into Caroline's house.

If Conor did kill McCarthy, why put the head in Caroline's basket? She'd tried to help him. But maybe Conor was an ultramacho man who viewed aid from a woman as an affront to his masculinity. Maybe dumping the head in her basket was his way of thumbing his nose at her, of declaring, "I don't want or need your help. I'll handle this my way."

Basile's words came back to me: "Now he's dead. Murdered. And all because he got on the wrong side of a psycho."

Had Caroline gotten on the wrong side of a psycho, too?

Before dialing Basile's number, I struggled to overcome my aversion to the man. If he'd reminded me of a cocker spaniel or even an Irish setter instead of a bloodhound, would I have liked him better? Probably. But as McCarthy's best buddy, he was a means to an end.

Basile answered on the first ring. I told him I wanted to talk about life insurance. He said he had the morning off and we arranged to meet at his apartment in a half-hour.

Located on the second floor of a nondescript low-rise brick building, Basile's apartment had all the charm of a motel room. The furnishings were cheap and minimal and Basile had added no decorative touches. No plants, no knickknacks or mementoes, no prints or posters, few books save a couple of paperback best-sellers, and no family photographs. Except for his computer and a stack of file folders containing insurance forms, Basile's desk was bare.

"I'm glad you've seen the light," he said over instant coffee that tasted like sludge. "Is it because of what I said about those kids on the overpass with the rocks? Or the crazy in the restaurant with the semiautomatic? Both incidents really happened. They're from a clipping file I keep of freak accidents, bizarre killings—things you'd never think would happen in a million years."

I kept a clipping file myself of odd bits of historical trivia—an effort to exhume the remains of John Wilkes Booth, the recovery of a stolen portrait of Thomas Jefferson. Maybe if I sold insurance instead of writing history texts, I'd clip the kind of stories Basile did but I doubted it. "It wasn't either incident, but what you said about McCarthy having a drink with friends when the phone rang and it was death calling."

"Mmmm." Basile removed a paper clip from a file folder on his desk and twisted it.

"You think his killer called to arrange a meeting?"

"I didn't hear their conversation," Basile replied. "But that call disturbed Ray. He left the bar soon after."

"Did he say where he was going?"

"Just that he had some business to take care of."

"I wonder who it was with," I mused aloud.

Basile was silent.

"The other night you said McCarthy had gotten on

the wrong side of a psycho," I pressed.

"Did I? I was so beside myself I barely remember." Basile sniffed and looked confused like a hound that's lost the scent.

"Just before you broke down."

He started to shake his head, then his expression cleared. He bent the paper clip into a straight line. "I must've been thinking of that Indian Ray got into a fight with."

"The Indian with the sign calling Myles Standish a murderer?"

"No, the guy standing next to him. Ray did go up to the Indian with the sign and give him hell. But then this big guy wearing sunglasses butted in and told Ray off. Gotta watch out for those guys with shades."

"Why?"

" 'Cuz nine times outta ten they're not wearing those glasses for protection. They're hiding behind them."

"Hiding what?"

"The craziness in their eyes." The paper clip pinged as it hit the wastebasket. Papers rustled on Basile's desk. "We're supposed to be talking about insurance, not crazy Indians. Here are some things you need to consider."

For the next fifteen minutes Basile explained "term," "whole life," "cash value," "annuities." "So what's it gonna be?" he said at last.

"I . . . uh. . . ." It hadn't occurred to me he'd want to close on the spot.

The phone rang. Basile picked it up and listened, frowning. He turned to me. "Client with a problem. Gonna take awhile to get it straightened out. Why don't you take these forms and get back to me?"

I said I would and let myself out.

Caroline answered my knock. The TV was tuned to *Sesame Street* and Eileen was on the phone. "Lunch sounds lovely, Nan. But I'm afraid we'll have to take a rain check."

I could tell from Eileen's tone that she was tempted by the invitation but felt duty-bound to refuse. "When Caroline's feeling better, I'll—"

"Have lunch with her," I interrupted, seeing my

chance for some time alone with my niece. "I'll stay here with Caroline."

"Excuse me a moment." Eileen covered the mouthpiece. "I'd like to but. . . ." She cast an appraising glance at Caroline, now sprawled on the bed in front of the TV.

"We'll be fine," I assured Eileen.

"Will you be all right here with Miranda?" Eileen asked. Caroline turned from the TV, fixing her gaze first on her mother, then me as if weighing which of us was the lesser of two evils. After more than twenty-four hours of her mother's company, the balance seemed to have shifted back in my favor. "Yes. Go!" she exclaimed, pointing at the door. Eileen looked hurt but also relieved at getting her walking papers.

After Eileen had gone, I sat on the bed next to Caroline. "Conor told me about his bet with McCarthy and how you offered to lend him money."

Caroline's eyes flicked from the screen where Big Bird and Mark Morris galumphed through a pas de deux to me. "When did you speak to him?"

"Last night. I ran into him as I was leaving the hotel."

"Lucky you." She returned her gaze to the TV.

"He thinks your quarrel with McCarthy was over the bet. Is that true?"

Caroline didn't reply. Big Bird and Mark Morris bowed to each other.

I tried again. "Were you afraid to tell about the bet because you thought it might look bad for Conor?"

Caroline remained silent. Big Bird and Mark Morris gave way to kids splashing in a swimming pool. *Jaws* music played ominously in the background. The music reached a crescendo as a huge letter *M* sprang like a shark from the water. Caroline and I gasped. I jumped up and switched off the set. "Plenty of people make foolish bets without—"

"No!" Caroline burst out. "Ray threatened Conor. He said if Conor didn't pay up, he'd see Conor went to jail!"

"But people don't go to jail just because they owe money. Debtors' prison was abolished a long time ago. Are you sure that's what McCarthy said?"

Caroline nodded fiercely.

I thought for a moment. "Maybe there wasn't any bet. Maybe McCarthy found out about something Conor did and was using it to blackmail him. Something serious enough to land him in prison if it became known."

I expected Caroline to protest but she didn't. She just looked miserable. She must've already figured this out for herself. I was about to ask why she hadn't told anyone, why she continued to protect Conor even now, when the answer hit me like a whack on the head. I plunked down on the bed again and put an arm around her shoulders. "You're in love with him, aren't you?"

Caroline turned crimson and nodded.

"But baby, you barely know him."

"I know I love him."

"But if he's done something wrong, if—"

"I knew you wouldn't understand!" Caroline flared. "That's why I didn't tell you. You don't know what it's like to—" She bit her lip.

"Really love someone?" I finished.

Caroline squirmed, refused to meet my eyes. "You and Simon. . . ."

She was floundering, digging herself in deeper. And suddenly I saw myself through her adolescent eyes—a fossilized forty-something and the former spouse in an overly polite, passionless marriage. "Weren't exactly Romeo and Juliet," I filled in. "Ever. But I did feel that way about someone once."

Caroline listened, wide-eyed, as I told her about my stormy relationship with Pat Landis, campus radical and Che Guevara look-alike. Pat of the clenched fist and shouted slogans, of long, sweet nights of lovemaking on a mattress on the floor at the East Paly house he shared with other comrades-in-arms.

When I was finished, she said, "But if you cared about him so much, why did it end?"

"He wanted too much too soon. I was supposed to break with family and old friends and drop out of school so I could devote myself to the revolution and him. When I didn't, he dumped me for someone else."

"Asshole," Caroline muttered to my astonishment. I hadn't thought that word was in her vocabulary. But then, as I was fast finding out, there was a lot I didn't know about my niece.

"Maybe. But I've never known anyone with so much energy, so much charisma, so much sheer animal magnetism. When he dumped me, I was devastated. Cried for weeks and begged him to take me back. I thought I'd never get over Pat."

"But then you met Simon?"

"We'd known each other since grade school. Our parents were friends, we lived in the same neighborhood, went to the same church. Simon was like an old shoe. Familiar. Comfortable. Safe. He listened and passed the tissue box while I carried on about Pat."

"What happened to Pat?"

"How should I know? I haven't seen him in over twenty years."

"You never tried to get in touch?" Caroline was incredulous.

"No. Why would I?"

"You must've at least thought about him from time to time."

"I've thought about him all right and wondered, too, but maybe I'd rather remember him as he was than find out he's become some fat, balding Silicon Valley CEO with a wife and three kids."

"Yuck!"

"Right. He'd lose all his romantic appeal, unlike your Conor who—"

"Don't start!" Caroline protested. "We don't know for sure he's done anything wrong. And even if he has, it can't be that bad."

I hoped for her sake it wasn't. "Caro—"

She pressed a finger against my lips. "Enough already. Let's get lunch. I'm starving."

At Caroline's urging, we went to the 1620 House, an English-style pub on Water Street, a short distance from the hotel. Caroline maneuvered us to a table near the entrance. Every time someone came in, she looked up eagerly, no doubt hoping for a glimpse of Conor. After the waitress had taken our orders, I risked a return to that prickly subject.

"When you and Conor walked to the lounge Saturday morning, did you try again to persuade him to accept the loan?"

"Yes."

"What did he say?"

"The same thing he'd been saying all along—that he wouldn't take it." Caroline eyed me suspiciously. "What are you getting at, Miranda?"

"Nothing."

"Oh yes, you are. You hope I'll say Conor told me he didn't need the money anymore because he knew Ray was dead. Well, he didn't say anything like that!"

"But you do admit Conor has a motive and that he had the opportunity to put the head in your basket when. . . ." I hazarded a guess. "When he went into your house at the village."

Caroline's stricken look told me my gamble had paid off. "Who told you that?" she demanded.

"Does it matter?"

"I have a good idea who. What if Conor was in my house? We walked to the village together and I asked him to come in. I was with him the whole time. I'd have noticed if he tried to sneak a head into my basket. Besides, he wasn't the only one to darken my doorstep that morning."

"Who else did?"

"Seth."

"What did he want?"

"He's a neighbor, so he often looks in on me. Beryl, too, though that morning Harvey dropped in. And Seth had a particular reason for stopping by."

"What was that?"

"He wanted to apologize for his behavior in the lounge."

"He mentioned that to me. What happened?"

Caroline frowned at her empty place setting. "Wish our food would come. I can't bear to eat while Mom's shoving food in my face. But now that she's gone, I'm ready to pig out. Where's our waitress? I don't see her anywhere."

"I'll find her but first tell me about Seth."

Caroline chewed a nail. "I'd gone into the women's dressing room to look for an extra coif for Nikki. When I came out, everybody had left for the village. But Seth was there."

"By himself?"

"Yeah. He must've just come in. Anyway, he looked like a wild man with his hair standing on end, shirt tail out, and a cut on his cheek."

I nodded, remembering.

"Guess I stared at him the wrong way," Caroline continued, "because he really lit into me. Demanded to know what my problem was. Said he was late but that wasn't a crime, was it? I know when to let well enough alone. I picked up my basket and went on my way."

My mind snagged on the scene of Caroline encountering wild-man Seth alone in the lounge. Wild-man Seth with a gym bag containing a hard object. I had a bruise on my leg to prove it. If that object had been a human head, he could've slipped it into Caroline's basket while she was in the dressing room. That would explain his lashing out at her; she'd nearly caught him red-handed. But why her basket? As far as I knew, Seth had nothing against Caroline. Perhaps he'd panicked and deposited his burden in the first available receptacle. Yet why kill McCarthy to begin with? McCarthy had shown him up but that was hardly a motive for murder. No, there had to be something more.

"Earth to Miranda," Caroline's voice broke into the jumble of my thoughts. "You said you'd check on our waitress."

"I'll go but. . . ." What was it I wanted to ask her? Mentally I reviewed what she'd told me so far and found a slight discrepancy. "If everyone had already left for the village when you came out of the dressing room, how'd you end up walking there with Conor?"

"I saw him ahead of me, called to him, and he waited. Now will you—"

"One more question. When did Seth come to your house?"

"Right after Conor left."

"What about Basile?"

"He came in a minute or two after Seth but didn't stay long. He noticed my kettle was empty and went to fill it with water. That's when Seth apologized. He said arriving late had put him in a bad temper. I told him it was no big deal. We talked for awhile longer, then Seth went back to his house, got the drum, and banged it in the street to call us to morning meeting."

"Did everyone show up for it?"

"Miranda! You said one more question."

"I'm going."

I found our waitress in the kitchen, arranging chunks of cheese and sausage on a plate for a Plowman's lunch. "Sorry for the wait," she apologized. "The cook got sick. I've had to help out here. Your order's next."

I returned to an empty table. I glanced quickly around. No Caroline. Heart racing, I rushed toward the entrance.

"Can't I go to the bathroom without you panicking?" Caroline called from behind me. "You and Mom are two of a kind." She shook her head with mock disgust. Then her expression changed to genuine annoyance.

"Mistress Allerton, well met!" Zack greeted her. "I had not thought to find thee here."

"Nor I, thee—you big snitch!" Caroline stormed past him out of the restaurant.

Mortified, Zack watched her go. He turned on me accusingly. "I can't believe you told her about our conversation this morning."

"I didn't."

"But—"

"I'll explain later." I hurried after Caroline, catching up with her at the passageway that led from Water Street through a cluster of small shops into the hotel parking lot.

"Did you have to do that?" I scolded.

"He blabbed about Conor's being in my house."

"So? You were with Conor the whole time and other people came in as well."

"Yeah, but he didn't mention them, did he?"

"Give him a break. He's got a huge crush on you and

maybe if you were a little nicer. . . ." I stopped. My mother had said the same thing to me in similar circumstances. And like me, Caroline made a wry face. "Okay. End of lecture," I said. "But now that we're out of there, what do you want to do about lunch?"

"Let's get a bite at the hotel."

As we made our way through the cluster of shops, I glanced in the window of a greeting card store and spotted Eileen fingering a cardboard cutout turkey centerpiece. Caroline saw her, too. "Uh-oh," she said. "Better hightail it back to the room before Mom sees us."

I caught Caroline by the arm. "Wait! Look at that!" The display case behind Eileen erupted in a multicolored shower of cards and envelopes. Nan Lowe stood at the center of the explosion, arms flailing frantically as if warding off an attack of killer bees.

14

> *"William Bradford being at work . . . was vehemently taken with a grief and pain. . . ."* Mourt's Relation

"What're you doing?" A young saleswoman caught Nan Lowe by the arms as Caroline and I rushed into the store.

Eileen spun around. "Nan, what's the matter?"

Nan looked from the clerk to Eileen, then at the mess at her feet. "I—I. . . ." Her voice quavered like a frightened child's. "I'm sorry."

"A dear friend of hers is ill and in the hospital," Eileen said softly to the clerk.

"That's no reason to tear the place apart," the clerk retorted.

"We'll help you put these back." Eileen stooped to pick up the cards.

"She can do it." Nan switched from humble to haughty. "That's what she gets paid for."

The clerk scowled.

"Naturally, I'll make good any damage I've done." Nan turned to go. "Send the bill to Mr. Seth Lowe on Jerusalem Road in Cohasset."

The elite address had the desired effect. "All right, Mrs. Lowe," the clerk replied deferentially.

We said good-bye to Nan at the entrance to the hotel. She did a good job of hiding it, but I could tell she was still shaken by the incident. Her lips moved angrily as she strode to her car. Caroline disappeared into the lobby. Eileen was about to follow when I detained her. "What happened to set her off like that?"

Eileen's face wore a bemused expression. "I don't know. She seemed fine all through lunch. Then on the way back to the hotel, she said she wanted to buy a get-well card for a friend and the next thing I knew she was ripping cards off the rack."

"Odd."

Eileen nodded. "How was it with Caroline?"

"Fine. She wanted some air so we went for a walk. I figured she'd work up an appetite that way, too."

"Good idea." Eileen beamed approvingly for the first time since her arrival.

The clerk was dusting off the last few cards when I returned to the store. "You should charge her for the aggravation alone," I remarked to show I sympathized.

She smiled. "Maybe I will. For that and the card she tore up."

"May I see it?" I asked on impulse.

"Help yourself." The clerk gestured toward a trash bin. I fished out the pieces and put them together on the counter. They showed a painting, done in the Impressionist style, of a young girl stretched out in a hammock. Sunlight filtering through tree branches glinted on her long blonde hair and cast a ruddy glow on her plump arms and shoulders, bare but for the pale yellow spaghetti straps of her sundress. A book lay open on the girl's lap, its green cover steepled over the mound of her belly. The girl's cheeks were flushed from either the sun or sleep, her lips parted in a drowsy, inviting smile. The artist had captured her freshness and beauty as well as the languor of the summer afternoon.

I turned the card over, searching for the artist's name. The back was blank. Odd. Usually a card like this provided information about the painting, the painter, and often the museum that owned the painting. There was nothing here, not even the name of the company that had manufactured the card.

Nikki had found note cards with a painting of a

blonde girl in a hammock at McCarthy's, I recalled. The girl in this painting did bear a slight resemblance to Caroline. But she resembled someone else more strongly. I studied the youthful face. If I did an age-progression like those done for children missing a number of years, whose face would I see? My age-progression had to take into account the passage of as many as thirty years, but before my eyes the soft girlish features became those of a mature woman.

"May I keep this?" I asked the clerk.

"Sure." She grinned. "Consider it a gift from Mr. Seth Lowe of Jerusalem Road, Cohasset."

Under the overcast early afternoon sky, the huge, dark-shingled house appeared more gloomy than grand. No light blazed in the windows as on the night of the party; no voices or sounds of laughter broke the stillness. The house might have been a mausoleum. When I rang the doorbell, the loud noise nearly made me jump.

The Lowes' West Indian maid answered the door and disappeared upstairs to fetch her employer. After a few minutes Seth Lowe came down, looking ruffled and agitated. "Sorry to keep you waiting," he said as he led me down the long hall, "but it's been one crisis after another."

We entered the library—a bibliophile's delight. The entire wall across from the entrance was lined with books, some obviously sets judging from the sameness of their leather-and-gilt bindings. A fireplace graced the front of the room and a slipcovered couch, whose rumpled cushions suggested that someone had been stretched out there recently, faced it. A high, narrow table stacked with larger-sized books stood behind the couch. In the rear was an easy chair and next to it a smaller table, also stacked with books.

"This is a wonderful room," I said admiringly.

"Thank you," Lowe replied. "Nan thinks it rather shabby, but I wanted a place where I could feel at home so I declared it off-limits for her decorator." Already he seemed more relaxed. "You'll find the books on the early exploration of the Americas over there." He motioned toward the rear shelves. "But before you get down to business, here's something you might enjoy. It arrived in the mail today."

Lowe handed me a package made of folded pieces of stiff cardboard and tied with string. I untied it. A musty smell filled my nostrils. I flushed with excitement. The leather cover was blackened with age. With extreme delicacy, as though parting the petals of a flower, I opened the book. Its pages were filled with woodblock-printed Gothic script. Drawings of plants and animals—some of them fantastic creatures—the sun, moon, and stars decorated the margins. My heart rate accelerated. I broke out in a sweat.

"It's a seventeenth-century almanac," Lowe said at my elbow.

I murmured appreciatively, then asked for a glass of water.

Lowe studied me for a moment. "Are you feeling all right? You look—is it book lust?"

"How did you know?"

Lowe smiled. "I've often fallen victim to it myself in libraries and rare bookshops."

He left to get my water. I glanced around the room, noticing for the first time a framed portrait of a Pilgrim on the wall over the mantel. When Lowe returned with a glass, I asked who it was.

"Edward Winslow. He's Nan's ancestor and the only Pilgrim to have his portrait painted."

Unwittingly, he'd provided me with an opening. "So Winslow started a family tradition of having one's portrait painted."

Lowe's eyes narrowed. "What do you mean?"

I removed the card, now taped back together, from my bag and placed it on the table. "This is Nan as a young woman, isn't it?"

Lowe seized the card and for a moment I thought it would be torn to pieces a second time. But as he stared at the picture, an expression at once fond and faraway came over his face. Whatever he felt for his wife now, it was clear that once he'd been deeply in love.

"When was this painted?" I asked.

"The summer before we met," Lowe replied without taking his eyes from the reproduction. "I was a junior at Yale, Nan a freshman at Vassar. I'd recently read Bradford's history of Plymouth Plantation and become fascinated with the Pilgrims. I was at a mixer and in walked this exquisite creature who turned out to be a *Mayflower* descendant. I'd never met anyone like her. From the moment I saw her, I pursued her shamelessly."

"I can see why. She was lovely."

"Yes." Lowe placed the card face down on the table.

I glanced at the blank back. "It doesn't give the artist's name."

"No, but you wouldn't have heard of him anyway," Lowe said quickly. "He was a local and very minor talent."

"I'd still like to know his name. We use a fair amount of art to illustrate the history texts I write and I'm always interested in learning about new artists, even lesser-known ones."

Lowe ran a hand through his shock of graying hair. "It's on the tip of my tongue, but I've forgotten."

"The painting belongs to your wife's family?"

"Actually, it's ours. It used to hang there." Lowe pointed to a place on the wall to the right of Edward Winslow. "Several years ago, I decided it would be safer elsewhere. It's an original painting; the picture of Winslow is only a print. There's a temperature-controlled vault in the basement of the Visitor Center at the village where we keep our collections of original furniture, paintings, and artifacts. I put the painting in storage there."

"This card was made before the painting went into storage?"

"I don't know when it was made," Lowe declared irritably. "It was done without my knowledge or approval."

"But why would someone do that?"

"To annoy us, of course. Nan told me about the incident. You were there; you saw how upset she was. She felt as if she'd been violated."

I'd be surprised and somewhat miffed to find my likeness on a greeting card, but I doubted I'd fly into a rage. "Nikki said she saw cards like this at McCarthy's. Do you think he could've—"

"Can we talk about something else?" Lowe interrupted. "You don't know what it's been like these past few days. If it's not the police, it's the visitors all day long, hammering away at us with their endless questions." Lowe seized a silver letter opener from the table and waved it in the air. "As if an interpreter would've—I don't know how many times I've pointed out to the police that anyone could've dressed up like a Pilgrim. Why, only last month we had these Mennonite visitors and nearly everybody mistook them for Pilgrims. As for security, well, kids often wander in after hours. Sometimes they take things. Sometimes we find things they've left behind. It would be easy enough for someone to—"

The letter opener flashed before Lowe's eyes and a look of astonishment came over his face. He put the instrument down and said in a calmer voice, "I'm rambling, I know, but given the pressure I—we've all been under. . . . It's a wonder you and Beryl were able to have a pleasant lunch yesterday."

"She told you about it?"

"A little. She mentioned you spoke about the hippie era at the village. Now that was an interesting time," he remarked, obviously eager to shift from recent events to the past.

"It did sound interesting," I agreed, wondering what he might add to Beryl's account.

"Yes," Lowe said thoughtfully. "Unfortunately, there aren't many of us left who remember it. Me, Beryl, Conor. . . ."

"Conor was at Plimoth then?" It was my turn to be astonished.

Lowe nodded. "Just for a season, I think. Or maybe only part of a season. I have a vague recollection he left abruptly before the season ended. Here one day, gone the next. Surprised me at the time because he enjoyed the work and was good at it."

"Why did he leave then?"

"I don't remember. You'll have to ask Conor. Or Beryl. She kept in touch with him over the years. When she heard he needed a job, she persuaded him to come back."

So Beryl and Conor were old friends. Pity I hadn't thought to inquire about him the other day over lunch. But then I hadn't known about the blackmail or about Conor's being in Caroline's house Saturday morning.

There was a knock at the library door. Lowe opened it and spoke briefly with the maid. I slipped the card with Nan's picture into my bag.

"I'm afraid I'm needed elsewhere," Lowe said, "but you're welcome to stay and browse."

"Thanks, but I have some errands to run for Caroline and her mother," I fibbed.

"Too bad," he said with genuine regret, "because I can't think of a better way to spend a dreary November afternoon." He gazed longingly at the shelves with their many-hued volumes.

"Another time perhaps?"

"Yes. Oh, and Miranda." He placed a hand lightly on my arm. It was long and narrow with tapered fingers, the smooth pale hand of a scholar, but also one capable of wielding a sharp instrument. "I'd appreciate it if you didn't mention the business about the card to anyone."

As I pulled out of the Lowes' driveway, I glanced back at the big gloomy house with its turrets and eyebrowed windows. A wraithlike figure appeared in a third-story window. The madwoman in the attic, I thought with a thrill of fear. The curtains came together in a rush. Nan vanished from view.

15

"... knowing our own weakness ... and still lying open to all casualty, having as yet (under God) no other defence than our arms, we thought it most needful to impale our town...." *Good Newes from New England*

Back at the playhouse, I removed the card with Nan's picture from my bag and stared at it. There was a story here, but I doubted I'd get it from Lowe or his wife. Nikki's discovery of similar cards at McCarthy's suggested his involvement. He'd worked as a security guard. He could've found the painting in the storage vault, noted the resemblance to Nan, and had the cards made up. Then he'd planted one where she was sure to find it. But why go to all that trouble?

I tried out a scenario featuring McCarthy and Nan as lovers and Seth as the jealous, murderous husband but quickly rejected it. Blackmail seemed more likely. If, as I suspected, McCarthy'd blackmailed Conor, he could've blackmailed Nan, too.

Then the painting on the card must be associated with a secret in Nan's past. That was why it was no longer on view in Seth Lowe's library. And that explained why Seth had "forgotten" the painter's name. He had, however, mentioned that the artist was local. There might be someone around who knew the artist. I picked up the phone book and found a number for the Plymouth Art Association. I got an answering machine and left a message.

I drummed my fingers on the coffee table: 3:30 P.M. I could still get in a few hours' work before joining Caroline and Eileen for dinner. I switched on my laptop and tried to summon the explorers of the New World, but questions about the painting and its possible connection to McCarthy's murder swirled in my brain. I'd no sooner pushed them aside than other questions rushed in.

What to make of Conor's sudden departure from the village in the seventies? Maybe his draft number had come up and he'd fled to Canada. But dodging the draft twenty-odd years ago didn't make Conor a criminal now. He must've done something else McCarthy had found out about.

Maybe the trivia game contained a clue after all. I picked up McCarthy's cheat sheet. Three rogues were mentioned here: Fells, Oldham, and Morton. Could one connect with Conor? Fells had impregnated a maidservant and run away with her. What was the contemporary equivalent of his crime—having sex with a minor and transporting her across state lines?

Oldham had plotted against the Pilgrims by attacking them in letters to England and stirring up other disaffected members of the colony. Could Conor have been involved in subversive activities?

Subversion figured in Morton's story as well. He'd sold guns to the Indians, who'd used them against the English and Dutch colonists. Was Conor a terrorist on the lam?

His crime couldn't be recent because he wouldn't risk the public exposure of playing a Pilgrim at Plimoth. But how long ago had it occurred? Before his stint at the village in the seventies? Or after? He'd attended St. Etienne College. I'd start there. I called the Plymouth Public Library, found out St. Etienne was located in Coureur De Bois on Michigan's Upper Peninsula, got the number, and dialed.

The school had no record of Conor Day.

With the winter solstice only a month away, darkness came early. The light was fading fast when I pulled into the parking area at Plimoth Plantation. Few cars remained and as I hurried into the Visitor Center, I met the last stragglers on their way out. "We'll be closing soon," the woman at the desk informed me.

Viewed from the top of the hill, the village houses huddled like sheep protecting themselves against predators. The palisade stakes cast long spearlike shadows across the empty main street. If the time just before daybreak was the witching hour, so, too, was this twilight time, when shapes bled into one another like watercolors in a wash turning murkier by the minute. A figure emerged from a house and stood on a strip of ground for the moment safe from impalement by the shadow-spears. An interpreter or a phantom Pilgrim who'd vanish at my approach?

Don't be silly, I scolded myself. As I headed down the hill, John Billington, a.k.a. Harvey Basile, lifted his sad, droopy face.

"Is Master Howland about?" I asked.

"I haven't seen him," Basile replied. Evidently he'd decided that with the village about to close, he could afford to drop his Pilgrim persona. "But you might check his house. Fifth one down on the left."

"Thanks."

"Done anything with those insurance forms I gave you?" he called after me.

"Not yet."

"Don't put it off too long. You never know."

Sandwiched between two larger dwellings, John Howland's house was small with a side entrance. I stepped inside. It was dark and deserted. I turned to go. A hand clamped on my shoulder. A scream caught in my throat.

"What're you doing poking around?"

A broad-brimmed hat shadowed his face, but I recognized the voice. "You scared the bejesus out of me, Zack."

"What're you doing here?"

"Looking for Conor."

"He's gone home. Why d'you want him anyway? Gonna tell him what a big snitch I am, too?"

"Please, I said I'd explain. I didn't tell Caroline the information about Conor came from you. She figured it out. And what if she is mad at you? She'll get over it."

"No, she won't. You were there. You saw the look

she gave me. And the contempt in her voice—she hates me!"

"Don't blow this out of proportion. Caroline'll come round."

"No, she won't—ever!" His voice shook. "It was bad enough when she was indifferent to me. But at least then I had hope. Now even that's gone. And all because of you!"

"You're making a mountain out of—" I tried to slip past him. He shoved me backward. My spine hit the doorway's sharp edge. I gave a cry of surprise and pain.

"You down there, Conor?" a voice called from above. Basile.

Zack hesitated before replying, "No. It's Zack."

"Come and give me a hand. Gotta loose board I want to fix before somebody gets hurt."

"We'll finish this later," Zack hissed in my ear. He started up the hill. I galloped toward the nearest exit.

At the foot of the wooden stairs that led to the main parking area, I stopped to catch my breath and collect myself. Zack wasn't the person I'd thought: a likeable "Liz" studies major with a cherub's face and a yen for Caroline. Now I saw him as a potential John Hinckley whose unhealthy obsession with my niece might lead to violence. If it hadn't already.

A shape detached itself from the shadows and loomed above me. With a sack slung over its shoulder, it resembled a humpbacked whale. Zack trying to cut me off at the pass? I called his name, trying to sound calm, though my voice came out high-pitched and scared.

Silence.

"All right, then, don't answer. But I've had it with your nonsense. I'm coming up now." I took a deep breath and began my ascent, fearful as Jack climbing the beanstalk with the giant waiting at the top.

"What nonsense?" The giant's voice was both mystified and amused.

I felt like a fool. It was probably a maintenance man with a bag of trash. "Nothing. I thought you were an interpreter."

"Nope. I'm from the other side of the stockade."

"What?" I was a few stairs from the top now, close

enough to make out the dark twin mirrors of his sunglasses.
Nate Barnes. I felt relieved but also slightly apprehensive. I
stopped, legs straddling two steps, striving for a bantering
tone. "What are you doing here? Isn't it a little late for a
demonstration?"

"So it is. But not for a delivery." He shifted the bag
on his shoulders. A pointed object protruded from one end.
I gasped. He chuckled. "No human body parts in here, if
that's what you're thinking. There's turkey feathers, antlers,
deerskin, hooves, and other stuff that's been in my freezer
since last fall. With hunting season about to begin, I need to
free up the space. And they can use these things over at the
homesite."

"Where?"

"Hobbamock's Homesite. Don't tell me you've never
visited it."

"Of course, I have. Many times," I added defensively.

Though less well known than Squanto, Hobbamock
had played an important role in preserving good relations
between the Pilgrims and the Wampanoag Indians. An
ambassador from the sachem Massasoit, he had lived nearby with his family. The replica of his homesite was located
in a clearing in the woods a short distance from the Pilgrim
village. It consisted of several bark-covered dwellings called
wetus. There Native American interpreters in native dress,
along with non-Native staff in uniforms, explained about
Wampanoag culture and history, and demonstrated native
crafts and cooking.

"Then you know that the Wampanoag Indian
Program uses stuff like this for artifacts," Nate went on.

"Right." I climbed the remaining stairs and was
about to slip past him when his arm swung out like a road
block. "Not so fast. Your niece owes me a call, remember?"

"You don't give up easily."

"You either."

"What do you mean?"

He shrugged. "Just a feeling I have. About your
niece—"

"She can barely talk to the police, let alone—"

"A hotheaded Indian?" he finished. "I'm sorry about

the other day. I was out of line banging on her door."

"And when you told off Ray McCarthy," I couldn't resist adding.

"Guy was a pain in the ass."

"And ended up dead."

The sack landed on the ground with a thud. He squared his shoulders and rocked forward on the balls of his feet, towering over me, no longer a humpbacked whale, but a bear on its hind legs. "Look," he growled, "I get into plenty of verbal slugfests without knocking off my opponents." Then as if realizing his posture suggested otherwise, he assumed a less aggressive stance. "Truce?"

"Sure, but?" I pointed at the turnstile of his arm.

"Sorry."

The turnstile dropped. I strode briskly to my car. His footsteps clattered on the stairs behind me. The footsteps halted. "I'm not such a bad guy once you get to know me."

I got in my car and slammed the door, more rattled by the encounter with Nate Barnes than I cared to admit. Pulling myself together, I reminded myself why I was here. I'd come looking for Conor and damned if I'd give up before I found him.

16

"But we had no sooner turned the point of the harbour, called the Gurnet's Nose . . . but there came an Indian . . . having his face wounded, and the blood still fresh on the same, calling to them to repair home, oft looking behind him, as if some others had him in chase. . . ." *Good Newes from New England*

Stupid. Stupid. Stupid. Why hadn't I remembered the road to Gurnet Point was only accessible to four-wheel-drive vehicles? I grimaced at the deeply rutted sandy track leading out to the Point from the Duxbury Beach parking lot. Without even front-wheel-drive, my ancient Peugeot wouldn't get farther than a few feet before the tires spun helplessly.

I paced the parking lot, empty except for my car and a battered pickup. I could reach the Point on foot, but it would be a long walk on a cold night. Pity Conor had an unlisted number and I hadn't been able to get it. I'd left a message on Beryl's machine and gotten yelled at by Nan, who'd warned me to keep my nose out of her business.

Maybe I should return to the playhouse and wait for Beryl to call back. Or try Caroline, though she wouldn't like my contacting Conor. But then I'd have driven here for nothing.

Noise on the beach attracted my attention. It was now dark, but a moon and a sprinkling of stars, together with light from the houses at the Duxbury end, revealed a tall, lean man and a yellow Labrador coming toward me.

Though full-grown, the dog frolicked on the beach like a puppy, pawing at the sand, searching for buried treasure. The Lab found a piece of driftwood and brought it back to his owner. The man feinted a toss in one direction, then another. Each time the Lab lunged toward the feint, checked himself, and returned. Finally the man sent the missile sailing into the water. The Lab dove in and emerged, dripping, with the stick.

I shivered at the thought of the frigid water. Yet the Lab had plunged in without hesitation. He was brave or foolhardy—like me rushing out here to confront Conor. But the dog looked happy as he bounded toward his owner.

I strolled onto the sand toward them. The dog ran at me and, before I could stop him, leaped up and licked my face, splattering me with seawater and saliva.

"Down, Charlotte!" The owner grabbed the dog by the collar. "Sorry about that. Two years old and as rambunctious as ever. Have to keep her in her crate while I'm away from home or she'd chew up the place."

A bandanna was tied around the man's head and his face had the wrinkled, leathery look of a beachcomber. Maybe he was one of the Point's few year-round residents and knew Conor. "You live out there?" I gestured toward the Point.

"No. Duxbury." He pointed the other way.

I heard the rumble of an engine as another car pulled into the parking lot. The driver cut the lights, but no one got out of the car. The beachcomber and I exchanged glances.

"Kids," he said. "Guess they've got to have someplace to go. And it'd be a cold squeeze on the dunes tonight." He released the Lab, who immediately took off toward the parking lot. The beachcomber turned in that direction, too. "Enjoy your walk, but keep an eye out. Tide'll be coming in soon."

My mind made up, I headed up the beach toward the Point. After several minutes, I glanced over my shoulder. Man and dog were distant shapes. Soon he'd go home, feed the dog, fix his own dinner, while I. . . . My resolution flagged. I felt alone and vulnerable. *Turn back*, an inner voice advised. I faltered. Behind me lay the lights of Duxbury and the familiar world of a man walking his dog, kids necking in a car. Ahead lay a cluster of dark, deserted houses and in one of the few that wasn't boarded up for the winter, a man with a mysterious past. Maybe this wasn't such a good idea.

I took a deep breath. Freezing air stung my nostrils. I caught a whiff of dank fur on my clothes and thought of the dog's icy plunge, of the exhilaration she must've felt as she came out with the stick—the exhilaration of the chase, of facing danger, of overcoming hardship in pursuit of the prize. An exhilaration I'd only experienced vicariously.

For years I'd written about adventurous spirits—explorers, soldiers, settlers, and reformers—people who'd braved unimaginable terrors to achieve their goals. I felt a sudden urge to prove myself worthy of them. If they could sail across a dark and perilous sea, push into the howling wilderness, face hostile armies and angry mobs, surely I could walk a strip of shadowy beach to confront one potentially dangerous man.

My shoes schussed in the sand. A wave slapped against the shore followed by the hiss of withdrawing water. Ahead, the pale aureole of the Gurnet Point Lighthouse shone through the clouds, a beacon to mariners and to me.

There must be other people on the Point I could turn to in case I ran into trouble with Conor. And that needn't happen if I played my cards right.

A twig snapped. I jumped. For heaven's sake, I scolded myself, stop acting like a scared rabbit. It was either the wind or a small animal. Still, I glanced nervously at the brush crowning the dunes. Nothing but a tangle of branches. Good.

Another snap. I stared hard at the dunes and this time saw something that made my heart thud.

That rounded shape over there—a boulder, a large piece of driftwood, or a crouching figure? I glanced back toward Duxbury, gauging how far I'd come. The town lights appeared distant while the beam of Gurnet Light loomed larger. I was more than halfway to the Point. Too late to turn around. But I felt a strong pull toward the man and dog, the necking kids. If there were kids in that car. My scalp tingled with fear. Had someone followed me?

I'd never make it to the beach parking lot. My only hope lay in reaching the Point. I quickened my pace, moving forward but also toward the ocean to distance myself from the dunes and danger. Out of the corner of my eye I saw a figure rise, run a couple of yards ahead, then drop to the ground again. My blood went cold, then my body as a wave hit me. Icy water drenched my sneakers and sweatpants up to the knees.

The tide was coming in. I'd be trapped in an ever-narrowing space between the ocean and my pursuer. I broke into a run. My wet shoes weighed me down, but I didn't dare stop to remove them.

The figure barreled across the beach at me. My feet pounded the sand, my heart and lungs pumped quadruple time. Yet I had the nightmarish sense of getting nowhere, of being stuck on a treadmill while every lope brought him closer. I could almost feel his breath on the nape of my neck. Desperate, I hurled myself forward. Too late. He tackled me, splatting me into the sand. I wriggled beneath him, trapped like an animal under the wheel of truck.

My head twisted toward his. Eyes glared through the slits of a ski mask. I screamed. He shoved my face into the sand. Wet grit ground into my skin and clogged my nostrils. I fought for air, but he pressed my face into the suffocating mass. My brain felt like a balloon about to burst.

A wave sent him sprawling but gripped me in a stranglehold of its own. My chest and throat constricted with the stinging cold. I rolled onto my side, struggling for breath. He came after me on all fours, clawing at me like a monster crab. I kicked and thrashed. My heel caught his jaw. With a grunt he fell back. I tried to scramble to my feet. He bulldozed into me, knocking me backward into the foaming water. Then he was on me like a slab of cement crushing my middle, paralyzing my legs. My arms flailed but couldn't stop the rock slide of blows.

Beneath me, the sand gave way. I was sucked into a dark hole. Sinking, I had a vision. A huge golden beast sprang into the air. A harsh cry echoed through the hole. Blackness spread like a giant ink blot.

17

"Then I called Hobbamock, and desired him to tell Massassowat, that the Governor, hearing of his sickness, was sorry for the same; and though, by reason of many businesses, he could not come himself, yet he sent me with such things for him as he thought most likely to do him good in this his extremity. . . ." *Good Newes from New England*

Something poked at me. Poked and whimpered. "Leave 'lone," I moaned. The poking continued. With difficulty I cracked an encrusted eyelid. The golden beast stood before me, its coat glowing as if on fire. I shut my eye. More poking. Reluctantly I opened both eyes. The golden beast had morphed into a yellow Lab.

"Charlotte!" a voice shouted. A light bobbed toward us followed by a running figure. The light grew larger until it encircled the dog and me.

"Oh my God!" The beachcomber's leathery face filled my line of vision.

My gaze shifted to the shadows beyond. "See . . . him?"

"Who?"

"Ski mask."

The beachcomber shook his head. "You're in shock. Let's get you to the Point and help." He wrapped his jacket around me. "Can you walk?"

"Sure," I slurred. But my legs had become sodden

logs. I could barely move. The beachcomber levered me up. I leaned heavily against him, half staggering, half letting myself be carried. The Lab bounded ahead, vanishing over the crest of the dunes. Moments later, she returned, fussed at us and dashed off again. With each step a jackhammer pounded my head. Our own progress was agonizingly slow. The Lab must've made at least a half-dozen round-trips in the time it took us to reach the nearest house.

The lights were on, but no one came in response to the dog's barks or the beachcomber's calls and knocks. He tried the door. Open. We entered a room filled with birds. A cloth hawk hung from the ceiling fan. Paper gulls flapped across the walls. Wooden and ceramic sea and shore birds perched on table tops and shelves. I blinked. Had we blundered onto the set of a Hitchcock horror flick?

"Anybody home?" the beachcomber called. There was no reply but from behind a door came the noise of a shower. The beachcomber banged on the door. "We need to use the phone. It's an emergency."

The water stopped. Seconds later, the door opened, letting out a cloud of steam. Conor emerged from the steam like a genie from a bottle. His russet hair hung in wet curls around his ruddy face. He wore a kelly green robe. The colors of his robe, flesh, and hair appeared unnaturally bright as in early Technicolor movies. Dazzled, I lifted a hand to shield my eyes.

"Christ! What happened to you, Miranda?" The color leached from Conor's face; he shrank from me in horror.

"My dog found her on the beach. Call nine-one-one and get blankets."

"Cell phone's out."

With an exasperated growl, the beachcomber headed for the door. "Look after her while I find a working phone." The dog followed at his heels.

"Don't leave!" I cried.

Too late. The door slammed.

Conor took a step toward me, his expression unreadable. I backed up against the couch. An awful clacking noise began. I squinted into the steamy bathroom, half expecting to see a set of gag teeth like the kind my brother had teased me with when we were kids. But it was my own teeth that were chattering uncontrollably.

Conor's fingers fumbled at my clothes. The wet garments clung to me like a second skin. My own fingers were useless stumps. I let him undress me, helpless as a baby in his hands.

Balmy air from the bathroom gusted over my naked flesh. I twisted in that direction like a plant straining toward the sunlight. But the tepid air couldn't melt my frozen core. I felt the truth of the expression "chilled to the bone." My teeth rapped out their SOS.

Conor grabbed an afghan from the couch and bundled me in it. His arms enveloped me. He hugged me tightly. A warning signal flashed in my brain but was quickly banished by my overwhelming need. I pressed against him, pores sucking greedily at the heat emanating from his body. I drew that heat into me, thawing my muscles, blood, and bones. My body relaxed, my teeth stopped their frantic noise. Like a cat before the fire, I basked in his warmth.

Then I felt as if someone doused the fire with water. Conor pushed me away. Cold air whooshed in between us. I barricaded myself in the afghan, but it offered scant protection against the ice in Conor's eyes and voice when he demanded, "Why the hell did you come out here?"

"To talk."

"Why didn't you telephone?"

"I couldn't get the number. Besides, your phone's out, isn't it?"

Conor said nothing. Outside, the dog barked. Conor leaned toward me, so close I could see the line of demarcation between the blue and brown parts of his eye. His lips grazed my ear. "Watch your step, Miranda. Next time you won't be so lucky."

18

"When any are visited with sickness, their friends resort unto them for their comfort, and continue with them ofttimes till their death or recovery." *Good Newes from New England*

My brother Martin and I paddled out to ride the waves on our inflatable rafts. He was in the lead and motioned for me to hurry up. I paddled furiously. A wave towered over us like a dark green sea monster. My heart beat with excitement and fear as first Martin's raft, then mine rode the long, sinuous neck.

"Made it!" I cried once we were safely over the crest. My brother turned to me, except it wasn't Martin anymore, but a stranger in a ski mask. Eyes glared through slits, an arm shoved my raft backward over the curl.

The raft flew from under me. An avalanche of water engulfed me, roaring in my ears, filling my lungs, bloating my brain. The wave pounded me to a pulp. Then, force spent, it dumped me on the sand.

I lay there, every muscle aching, gasping like a grounded fish. Beneath me, I felt the seaward tug of the tide and was tempted to let it sweep me away. But a voice, faint at first, then louder and more insistent, called my name, "Miranda, wake up!"

I opened my eyes and peered into Eileen's violet ones, dark-circled like a badger's. "Where. . . ?"

"It's all right now," she soothed, stroking my hair. "You're at the playhouse. On the floor actually. You were having a nightmare and rolled off the futon. Here, let me help you up." She eased me back onto the cushion.

"But how did I get here?"

"You telephoned from the hospital and we came for you. Don't you remember?" Her face was filled with concern.

"No—yes, I think so." After some digging, I unearthed shards of memory.

I'm lying on a gurney under the unforgiving glare of fluorescent lights. The words "head injury" and "hypothermia" hang in the disinfected air. There's a doctor and before him, two EMTs, whose efficiency belies their youthful appearance. A jouncing ride. And somewhere along the way, a policeman. Not Navarro—this one's eyebrows are blessedly benign. He nods and jots things down. I must be talking to him but I can't hear a word I say. At some point I sneak off to phone my parents, an unwilling Candy Striper who can't wait until her four-hour stint is finished.

I turned my attention back to Eileen. "What time is it?"

"Almost 9:00 A.M. Can I get you anything?"

Her voice exuded empathy; as a caregiver she was in her element, tending to me like a sick child. And this time I was grateful for her solicitude. "Coffee would be great."

"I'll have to go out for it," Eileen said. "Caroline hasn't done much grocery shopping lately. Will you be okay while I'm gone?"

I nodded.

"Make that two coffees," Caroline called from the loft above. "And chocolate donuts."

"Her appetite's coming back," Eileen whispered. "Back in a jiffy."

Eileen was barely out the door when a pair of long, slender legs slid down the ladder. Clad in an oversized tee shirt with a mayflower—the flower not the ship—Caroline plopped down on the floor in front of me, pulling her legs to her chest and propping her chin on her knees. "Jeez, Miranda, are you all right?" Her concern mirrored her mother's.

I smiled wanly. "I've been better."

"What happened? Why did you go to Duxbury Beach?"

"I was on my way to see Conor."

Her chin jerked up from her knees. "Miranda! I never should've told you about him and Ray."

"It's not only that. Yesterday Seth Lowe let slip that Conor worked at the village in the early seventies."

"So?" Her chin dropped back onto her knees.

"He left abruptly before the season ended. Seth didn't remember why."

"I still don't see why that's important."

"He lied to me about where he went to college."

Caroline's head disappeared behind her legs. "What's the big deal?"

"I'm going to find out."

"Don't, Miranda. Please."

"Conor told me to back off, too."

"But I thought—when did you speak with him?"

"The man who found me brought me to Conor's house. Conor was in the shower. Maybe warming up after attacking me on the beach."

"Miranda!" Caroline's head shot up again. "Was he expecting you?"

"I don't know. Someone could've alerted him. He claimed his phone wasn't working, but I'm not so sure about that."

Caroline sprang to her feet. "It couldn't have been Conor then. It was probably some weirdo who preys on women."

I wished I could've believed that. But I couldn't dispel the suspicion that my attacker had been someone I knew—if not Conor, then another person who'd followed me to the beach.

We were down to donut crumbs and coffee dregs, and I felt less like something that had washed ashore when Navarro and another man showed up.

Eileen greeted them at the door. "Are you here because Miranda was attacked last night?"

Navarro and his companion exchanged surprised

glances. "This is the first I've heard about it." Navarro's brows beetled at me.

I described briefly what had happened. Navarro asked a few questions and expressed concern for my well-being but soon made it clear he had other fish to fry. "Larry," he said with a nod at his companion.

The other man stepped forward. With his neatly trimmed silver goatee, thick glasses, tweed jacket, and battered briefcase, he looked like an academic but introduced himself as Detective Larry Pappas of the Boston Police. "Ray McCarthy used to be one of us, so the Plymouth police have asked for our assistance in their investigation. I'd like you both to look at some pictures and see if you recognize anyone," he said to Caroline and me.

We sat on the futon, Pappas in the middle and Caroline and I on either side. Navarro stood opposite, eyebrows trained on Caroline and me like antennae ready to catch the faintest glimmer of recognition. Eileen posted herself by Caroline.

Pappas placed a sheaf of photos on the coffee table. He picked up the top one and handed it to Caroline. After a quick glance, she shook her head and gave it back. He passed it to me. The grim person in the picture didn't look like someone I'd want to meet on a dark street alone. But then I felt the same way about my driver's license photo. I shook my head slowly. The back of my skull began to throb again. Pappas slid the photo to the bottom of the pile and repeated the process.

"Who are these people?" Eileen asked.

"Some folks McCarthy put behind bars awhile back."

"But if they're in jail, what's the problem?"

"They're out now."

"You think one of them killed him?" Eileen demanded.

Pappas shrugged. "It's a possibility." He gave Caroline another picture. As she took it, her gaze strayed anxiously to the one just uncovered. Her hands were trembling. Why? She should be relieved. Now that the police had broadened their investigation to include people from McCarthy's days as a Boston police officer, the pressure was off Caroline and her fellow interpreters. But not if one of the interpreters had been known to McCarthy the cop. That must be the reason for her distress: she was terrified of seeing Conor's face in this rogues' gallery.

Finally only two photos remained—one in Caroline's hand, the other face up on the table. Neither was of Conor, though. . . . I leaned across Pappas to get a better look, straining stiff muscles. Caroline sagged with relief. The photo she was holding floated to the floor. I reached for it. Stars flashed before my eyes. I sank back. Pappas retrieved the photo and handed it to me.

A boyish face stared at me, younger, more alert, his hair cropped too short to require combing. I remembered how he'd deplored the violence kids today were exposed to and how he wanted to expose his own to something more wholesome. "This one."

Caroline and the others looked at me with amazement. Navarro snatched the photo from my hand. "When?"

"Saturday morning at the village. But he had a baby in a Snugli and a toddler with him, so I don't see how he could have done it."

"Fine. We'll question them, too." Navarro started for the door. Pappas thanked us for our help and advised me to avoid deserted beaches until they got their man.

When the police had gone, Caroline flung her arms around me. "Take it easy," I protested, jolted by the force of her embrace.

"Sorry, but that was fantastic!"

"I don't—" I stopped, reluctant to rain on her parade. Why repeat the doubts I'd voiced to the police when Caroline desperately wanted to believe otherwise—that McCarthy's killer was not someone she knew, but a total stranger.

Looking happier than I'd seen her since my arrival in Plymouth on Friday, she jumped up. "C'mon, this calls for a celebration! Let's have music, dance. Put on a CD, Mom."

Eileen stared wonderingly at Caroline, puzzled by her sudden transformation. Then a smile broke over Eileen's face. I was reminded of something she'd told me a long time ago. "You know the song, *You Are My Sunshine?*" she'd said. "That's how it is with Caroline and me. When she's happy, I'm happy. When she's sad, I'm sad."

Now, basking in the glow of Caroline's newfound radiance, Eileen went over to the CD player. She'd barely slipped a CD into the slot when the phone rang. Caroline grabbed the receiver eagerly, perhaps hoping for more good news. "It's for you, Miranda." Her voice betrayed her surprise and disappointment. "Dottie Pierce from the Plymouth Art Association."

19

"But at length she discovered the thing, and prayed him to forgive her; for Lyford had overcome her and defiled her body before marriage. . . ." *Of Plymouth Plantation*

A tall regal woman in her seventies with iron gray braids arranged in a coronet on top of her head, Dottie Pierce was all business. In one hand she hefted a hammer, in the other an oil painting of Plymouth Harbor. Framing hooks jutted from her mouth. She put down the hammer and removed the hooks to greet me. "I'm afraid you've caught me at a bad time. My assistant just phoned in sick and I've got an exhibit to mount before the opening reception tonight. I can only spare a few minutes. What did you want to see me about?"

I showed her the card with the painting of Nan Lowe.

Dottie Pierce stared at the card with disbelief. "Why, it's one of Laurie's paintings of Nancy! Wherever did you get this?"

When I told her, she said, "So Seth's been holding out on me after all."

"What?"

Dottie Pierce rested the oil painting she'd been holding against a wall before answering. "After Laurie died, I wanted to exhibit his work."

"Laurie is. . . ?" I interrupted.

"Sorry. I always forget that most people have never heard of him. You'd have to have grown up around here like I did. Anyway, Laurie is—or rather was Laurence Stearns White. A landscape painter of minor repute, though he did do some first-rate pictures of his daughter."

"Nan?"

Dottie nodded.

I let this sink in. Seth had lied through his teeth when he said he didn't remember the painter's name. But why? Nan's secret must have something to do with her father. "You said Seth had been holding out on you?"

"Laurie gave the painting on this card to Seth and Nan as a wedding present. When I asked if I could borrow it for the exhibit, he told me it had been ruined while he had restoration work done."

Another whopper. Again I wondered why, especially since the painting showed Nan at her loveliest. "You mentioned Laurie did other paintings of his daughter."

"A series from the time Nancy was fourteen until she was eighteen. Laurie took them with him when he went to live abroad after he and Vivian—Nancy's mother—divorced. I wanted to exhibit them also, but I was told they'd been destroyed in a fire in Laurie's studio just after he died. It's a great pity those paintings didn't survive because they represented Laurie's finest work, even if some people found them disturbing."

"Disturbing?" I repeated, more intrigued than ever.

Dottie humphed as if to show she disagreed with this opinion. But instead of elaborating, she announced, "Time's up. If I don't get back to work, I'll have a bunch of disgruntled artists on my hands." Seizing hammer, framer's hooks, and canvas, she marched over to a far wall, held the painting up, and frowned. "What do you think? Too low?"

To my uncritical eye, the painting's position looked fine. But I saw an opportunity to engage Dottie in further conversation. "Maybe," I said. "Would you like me to hold it so you can see?"

"If you don't mind." Dottie gave me the painting and studied its placement. "A little more to the left." I moved it an inch. "Too far." I moved the painting back a bit, hoping this wouldn't go on too long. The painting was heavy and my arms were still sore.

Dottie squinted at the painting for a long moment. "That's it," she declared to my relief. While she marked the spot with a pencil, pounded in a hook, and hung the painting, I shook out my arms. Then I brought the conversation back to Laurence Stearns White. "If the other paintings of Nan were anything like the one on the card, I can't imagine why people would be upset by them."

"They weren't all like it," Dottie replied. I waited for her to continue. Instead she pointed to another canvas. "That goes next to the one I just hung."

Dottie was no fool; she knew she had a willing helper provided she kept the trickle of information flowing. My arm muscles protested but I did her bidding, jockeying the painting back and forth until Dottie pronounced herself satisfied and pounded in the hook.

"What were the other paintings of Nan like?" I asked.

Dottie studied a third canvas of young children frolicking on a beach, painted in the manner of Mary Cassatt. Her gaze flicked from the canvas to a spot on the wall as if she were mentally placing it. Then she turned to me and said, "Some were nudes. Nan being Laurie's daughter, people were shocked. There was nasty talk. Laurie already had a reputation as a lady-killer and Nan was a lovely girl."

So that was it. The rumor of abuse hung in the air between us, ugly but uncorroborated. Dottie, I suspected, could either dismiss this rumor or give it substance—if that was what I wanted. Having started down this path, I might as well follow it to the end. I shook out my arms, steeled myself for another lifting.

"We'll do this one next," Dottie said, indicating the Cassatt-like children. I hefted the painting, the heaviest so far, and held it against the wall, my face so close that I saw the individual daubs of paint on a little girl's bare legs. "Higher," Dottie ordered. I strained upward. "No. Too far. Down and to the right."

My arms ached. Paint daubs danced before my eyes. Still, I went on repositioning the painting until Dottie was finally content. After she moved in with her pencil and marked the spot, I rested, balancing the painting like a babe on my hip. "Do you think there was any truth to the gossip?"

Dottie paused, hammer upraised. "Who knows? Laurie's dead and if there is a dark secret in Nancy's past, she's not going to blab it to some talk show host or rush into print like so many silly fools these days." She banged in the hook and turned to me. "But I will say this. The summer Laurie painted her in the hammock, Nancy'd put on a lot of weight. Some people said it was baby fat."

The painting wobbled on my hip. I grasped the gilt frame more tightly, steadying it and myself in the wake of this none-too-subtle hint. Poor Nancy. Sympathy for the abused girl softened my dislike of the woman she'd become. Now I understood why McCarthy had written "daughter= concubine" on the cheat sheet for the trivia game. It was Nan's incestuous relationship with her father that McCarthy had hinted at with the story of Mr. Fells and his maidservant/concubine. That was the secret he'd threatened to reveal if the Lowes didn't pay his price. Still, it was hard to believe he'd blackmailed them on the strength of a painting and some old rumors. He must've found something besides the painting. Some definite proof.

Without realizing it, I must have loosened my grip on the frame because the next thing I knew, it slipped from my fingers. If Dottie hadn't caught the painting from below, the frolicking children would have crashed to the floor.

"Sorry!"

Dottie didn't answer. She propped the painting against the wall and examined it carefully. "Not your fault," she said. "Part of the frame's loose. I'm taking this back to Sylvan. I warned Gertrude not to go to him. He used to do good work but lately he's gotten sloppy." She traced the crack between the frame and the canvas and a wistful expression came over her face. "No billet-doux for you this time, Dottie my dear," she murmured.

"Pardon?"

Dottie returned from the distant place she'd been. "Laurie had a charming habit of hiding love notes between

the frame and canvas of paintings he gave his lady friends."
She picked up the painting with a fond smile. She had her
memory and I had my answer—one that gave the Lowes a
motive for murder.

Two glum faces greeted me upon my return. Eileen sat by the
phone, stretching the cord of the receiver in a futile effort to
straighten its many coils. Slouched in the butterfly chair,
Caroline performed a similar action on her wavy hair.

"What's the matter?" I asked.

"Martin—Nikki," they blurted simultaneously.

"You first, Mom," Caroline conceded with ill grace.

"Martin says he can't possibly get away until
Thursday. That's two whole days from now!" Eileen's voice
rose hysterically.

I felt a flash of sympathy. Playing supermom to an
uncooperative teenager was taking its toll. And on top of
that, she'd spent a sleepless night watching over her errant
sister-in-law. "I'll talk to him." Eileen handed me the phone
with a dubious expression.

Instead of arguing, I let Martin vent. When he ran
out of wind, I said, "I'm picking you up at Logan Airport
tomorrow afternoon." Then I hung up.

A moment later, the phone rang. "All right, but be on
time," Martin conceded.

"Well done, Miranda." Eileen beamed. "But are you
sure you're up to it? Wouldn't it be better if Caroline and I
met him?"

"I'll be all right. I'll drive back to Cambridge tonight,
take care of things there, then go to the airport tomorrow."
I turned to Caroline. "What's this about Nikki?"

"She called to say the coroner has released Ray's
body. The wake is this evening, funeral tomorrow." Caroline
tugged at her hair. "Mom doesn't want me to go."

Caroline and Eileen looked up at me like expectant
children, each hoping I'd take her side. "She's probably
right, Caro," I said finally.

"But everyone from the village will be there. Those
people are my friends. I hate not seeing them."

"I know but one of them may still have. . . ." I left

the sentence unfinished but Caroline got the message. With an angry, wounded look, she cocooned herself in the butter-fly chair in a reverse metamorphosis from butterfly to chrysalis.

20

"If they die, they stay a certain time to mourn for them. . . . in a most doleful manner, insomuch as though it be ordinary and the note musical, which they take one from another and all together, yet it will draw tears from their eyes, and almost from ours also." *Good Newes From New England*

I hadn't intended to go to the wake. But after a couple of Advils, a long, hot shower, and an even longer nap, I felt ready to face the world again. So, on the off chance the murderer would betray himself at this gathering, I stopped in at Long's Funeral Home before heading back to Cambridge.

A stocky man in a Pilgrim costume with a bandaged hand was signing the book when I walked in. Zack no sooner noticed me than he started to slink away like a villain in a Jacobean drama. I caught up with him.

"Uh, Miranda," he began awkwardly. "I didn't expect to see you here."

"Why not?"

"It's not like you—I mean you barely knew Ray," he fumbled. Then with a hopeful glance over my shoulder, he asked, "Is Caroline coming?"

I shook my head. "Not to the wake or the funeral."

"Oh." His face fell.

"What happened to your hand?" I asked, indicating the bandage.

"Hurt it when I was helping Harvey at the village."

The bandaged hand disappeared into his pocket. Avoiding my eyes, Zack said, "Sorry about last night. I was mad upset."

"Right."

The hand worked in Zack's pocket. He jerked his head toward the long, thickly carpeted hallway behind us. "Well, guess I'd better go pay my respects."

"Just a minute." I touched his elbow. "Did you go straight home after you left the village last night?"

"I stopped at McD's for dinner, then—why the third degree?"

I shrugged. "Make any calls from there?"

Zack's hand burrowed deeper into his pocket. "I don't know what you're after, but count me out. I'm not answering another question." He turned and hurried down the hallway. He may have had nothing to do with last night's attack on me, but he certainly acted guilty as all get-out.

I followed Zack into a large room. Against the wall nearest the entrance was McCarthy's coffin, awash with floral arrangements and thankfully closed. Nikki and Basile stood to one side. Her eyes were red-rimmed; his features sagged with sorrow. I couldn't decide which looked more despondent, the basset or the escapee from the *Addams Family Chronicles*. I wondered if Nikki had found out about her former boyfriend's whereabouts on the night of the murder, but now was hardly the time to ask. Reluctant to intrude on their coffin watch, I moved to the middle of the room, glancing around for familiar faces.

People were clustered in small groups, the interpreters distinguishable by the long hair, beards, and earrings on the men, and by their costumes. Zack spoke with a female interpreter. Seth Lowe was deep in conversation with Beryl, Nan nowhere in sight. Had she already come and gone? Or did her absence from the wake of a man she'd detested show she was less of a hypocrite than some of the others? Conor, I noted, wasn't present either. For the same reason?

Seth looked up and caught my eye. Anger suffused his scholarly face. Dottie Pierce must have told him about my visit and the questions I'd asked. Too bad. I liked Seth

and felt that under other circumstances we might have
become friends. Now he looked ready to storm over, but
Beryl's restraining hand kept him in place.

I glanced away. Besides the interpreters, there were
other groupings of clean-shaven men in suits and ties and
women in skirts and heels, who must be family, friends, and
colleagues from McCarthy's days with the Boston Police
Force. Detective Pappas was talking to a woman wearing a
huge black wide-brimmed hat. I guessed she was
McCarthy's ex-wife from the way people came over to offer
condolences. A trio of stony-faced teenagers, two boys and
a girl, lurked at her left.

I spotted Navarro alone in a far corner of the room
where he had a good view of everyone. He acknowledged
my presence with a lift of his eyebrows before training his
antennae elsewhere.

Pappas strolled over to me. "Ms. Lewis, we meet
again," he said pleasantly. "Here by yourself?"

"My niece and her mother decided not to come."

Pappas nodded. "Your niece seemed shaky this
morning. But thanks again for the positive identification."

"Did you pick him up for questioning?"

"He's left town but we'll find him."

"You can bet on that!" A red-faced man with the
beginnings of a paunch joined us. Pappas introduced him as
Sergeant Jack Rooney.

"You one of the actresses, Ms. Lewis?" Rooney
asked.

"Interpreters," Pappas corrected.

"Whatever. Are you?"

"A relative," I said.

Pappas whispered in Rooney's ear. I caught the
words "her niece." Rooney shook his head. "Of all the sick
things to do to a young girl. Grisly way to go, too," he
added with a glance at the coffin. "Should've stayed on the
force. He'd have been a lot safer."

"Why did he leave?" I asked.

Pappas glanced at McCarthy's ex-wife and lowered
his voice. "He was involved in a shooting that. . . ." He
tugged thoughtfully at his goatee, weighing what to say. His

beeper went off. Excusing himself, Pappas rushed toward the nearest exit where Navarro met him. They disappeared. Perhaps they'd gotten a lead on the whereabouts of the man I'd identified.

Rooney seemed to think so. He watched them go with an approving look. "Can you tell me why McCarthy left the BPD?" I asked.

Rooney cleared his throat, turned redder than before. "Like Larry said, he was involved in a shooting that—hell, I'm not comfortable with this. People hear about one guy who went berserk, they think all cops are alike." Excusing himself, he rejoined a group of colleagues.

I stared after him. *What* had McCarthy done?

"Are you all right, Miranda?" Beryl Richards's weathered apple face was etched with concern. "Conor told me about the attack on you and I'm so sorry. I feel . . . well . . . responsible."

Responsible? Why feel that? Unless Conor were my attacker and she'd been the one to warn him I was looking for him. "What do you mean?"

"If I'd been at home when you telephoned, I could've given you Conor's number and you never would've gone out there."

"His phone wasn't working."

"Oh." Beryl seemed surprised.

"Since I wasn't able to talk to him and he's not here now, maybe you can help me."

"Me? How?"

"Seth told me Conor worked at the village in the seventies but left abruptly before the season ended. Do you remember why?"

Beryl's fingers fluttered to the paisley scarf knotted around her neck. "That was a long time ago and we've always had a lot of turnover at the village."

"But you kept in touch with Conor," I persisted.

"Please," Beryl said softly, "some things are best left alone." She rubbed her neck as if the scarf had become painfully tight.

I decided not to press further. "Perhaps you're right." Beryl's fingers dropped from her scarf; she looked relieved.

Nearby someone sobbed. Nikki was crying into the crook of Basile's arm. Conor stood in the doorway, watching. He looked as if he wanted to comfort Nikki, but something held him back. In another time and place a person who resembled Conor had stared at me like that. But where, when? I struggled to remember.

And then the long-suppressed memory swept into my consciousness. "Conor was at Pat's!" I blurted.

"What?" Beryl looked at me with astonishment. Conor's head swiveled toward us. His eyes locked with mine just as they had that long-ago afternoon. Then he vanished.

21

"Instead of records and chronicles, they take this course. Where any remarkable act is done, in memory of it . . . they make a round hole in the ground . . . which when others passing by behold, they inquire the cause and occasion of the same. . . ." *Good Newes from New England*

I thought I'd be glad to be back in my Cambridge apartment, far from Zack, Conor, Nan, Seth, and all the rest. But the minute I walked in the door, I felt a curious sense of letdown. The place looked dingy and depressing. Was this what my life had come to? I pressed the button on my answering machine. One friend had called, but the other messages were from my editor on *America, the Republic's Glory and Greatness*, asking about the chapter that was due last Monday.

Ordinarily, this would have driven me straight to my laptop. Instead I fussed about the apartment, avoiding work but unable to shut out the memory etched in acid. Even now after so many years, it scorched my cheeks with shame.

I'm standing in front of the East Paly house Pat shares with his comrades-in-arms. My knuckles are raw from banging on the door, my voice hoarse from screaming. I know they're in there and it's killing me. Pat and Susan, his new love. Jealousy devours me like a pack of jackals. I want to rip them apart and take her place on the mattress. But the door is locked. No one comes. Finally I walk away. I'm

*halfway across the crabgrass lawn when something makes
me turn around. The curtains are parted. Someone is watching me from the front window. A stranger, no one I've ever
seen before. Our eyes lock for a long moment, then the curtains flap shut and he's gone.*

Could Conor really be the person I'd seen in the window two decades ago? Pat might remember him. I reached
for the fat red Stanford alumni directory. I'd opened it to
Pat's listing so many times the book automatically cracked at
that place. I hadn't had the guts to contact him all those
other times and I still didn't. Asking him about Conor might
lead to humiliating admissions I wasn't willing to make, even
now. Beryl was right, some things *were* best left alone.

What was Conor doing at the house that afternoon?
Was he a cohort of Pat's in the radical movement at
Stanford? I'd known that crowd and I didn't remember him.
Maybe he was just passing through. But where had he come
from and where had he gone? To Plimoth Plantation, where
he blended in with other hippie/Pilgrims? Then he'd left
abruptly. Running from what?

Establishing a chronology might help. I had a good
head for dates—it was one of the reasons I'd become an historian. My affair with Pat had begun in the winter of my
freshman year. By the following fall, the fall of 1970, Pat had
dumped me for Susan. So it must've been around then I'd
glimpsed Conor in the window.

Nineteen seventy. A time of turmoil at Stanford with
strikes, demonstrations, and destructive fires. The year of
Kent State, too? I flipped through an American history text,
stopping at an icon of the times—the photo of an anguished
young woman kneeling beside a slain student. The shooting
at Kent State had taken place in May 1970. There'd been
demonstrations on campuses throughout the country to
protest the invasion of Cambodia. And the following fall,
Conor had showed up at Pat's. What if. . . ?

My skin prickled with excitement. I might be close to
unraveling the mystery of Conor's past. But I needed more
information. I glanced at my watch. Eight-forty-three.
Luckily, the public library was open until nine, the main
branch nearby.

I ran the short distance, tore up the steps, past the main desk, into the reference section. The computers were down, but I spotted several fat blue *Facts-on-File* volumes on the shelf. Only those for recent years were there, but the librarian told me that earlier volumes were located on the fourth floor in the stacks. I entered that musty enclave where I'd spent many an hour happily browsing and climbed the metal stairway to the fourth floor. Locating the volume for 1970, I looked under Vietnam and was referred to Indochina.

"We'll be closing in ten minutes so please check out your books," a librarian announced over the PA system.

I scanned the first entries under "Domestic Reaction and War Protests." Footsteps clattered on the level below. A librarian or someone else? Last night's attack had made me jittery. Silly to believe my assailant had followed me here. Still. . . .

The footsteps came closer. If I peered down through the metal slats, would I see a man in a ski mask? With a finger snagged in the volume, I fled to the rear of the stacks. The footsteps ascended. I slid down the backstairs to level three and read a few more entries before descending to level two. When I heard the footsteps above me, I scudded to the basement.

The lights had been turned off, but I didn't dare flip a switch. I cowered in the shadows between two sets of stacks, heart thumping, finger crushed between pages. The footsteps reached the basement and stopped. I held my breath. They ascended to the next level and faded away. I counted slowly to ten before flipping on the light. The sudden brightness made me blink. I breathed deeply to calm myself. Then I read the remaining entries under "Domestic Reaction and War Protests."

I left the stacks and reached the main entrance just as a librarian was locking up. As I approached the door, an alarm went off. The librarian flashed me an accusing look. Chagrined, I handed over the blue volume. "Sorry," I apologized. He glared at me, implacable as a prosecutor. "That was wrong!"

Back at my apartment, I jotted down what I'd

learned. Two bombings and a deadly break-in had occurred in the summer of 1970. The bombings had been at the induction center in Minneapolis and the Wisconsin Army Research Center; the break-in, in which the night watchman had been killed, had been at the National Guard Armory in Ann Arbor. Tomorrow I'd find out if Conor had been involved in any of these incidents.

I was exhausted but sleep eluded me. I lay awake for a long time, twisting and turning to find a comfortable position. Finally I drifted into an uneasy slumber.

The loud report of a rifle, then a piercing wail. Someone's hurt. Caroline? Sick with fear, I join the others stampeding toward the noise. Then I see them, freeze-framed as in a photo: Caroline with her mouth open in a silent scream, her arms outstretched, begging for mercy. Too late. Smoke curls upward. A figure lies crumpled on the ground. Myles Standish shoulders his musket. "Murtherer," someone hisses from behind. But when I turn around, there's only empty air.

I jerked awake, clutched my right leg to control the spasm ripping through my calf muscles. When the spasm passed, I eased into a sitting position. My heart pounded, my head ached, and my flesh burned. It was just a dream, a crazy quilt incorporating bits and pieces of the past few days. Caroline had become the horrified young woman in the Kent State shooting, Myles Standish, or rather Ray McCarthy, the National Guardsman with the deadly aim. My unconscious had mixed things up. McCarthy was the victim, not the killer.

But maybe he was both. He'd been involved in a shooting serious enough to force his resignation from BPD. Had his murder been an act of revenge, after all? The police seemed to think this was a possibility. Otherwise, they wouldn't have come round with the mugshots of criminals McCarthy had put away.

Whoa! I'd gone to bed in pursuit of one suspect only to wake up on the trail of another.

Nothing happens by accident, my old therapist used to say. Once I'd gotten stuck in traffic and missed our appointment because, according to her, I wanted to avoid her and the unpleasant truths she made me face. So she'd charged me for the missed appointment.

Although I hadn't agreed with her, I questioned my motives now. Was I abandoning Conor because I didn't really want to know what he'd done, just as I shied away from acknowledging that Pat might've committed crimes I couldn't condone?

But I'm not turning back, I told myself. I'm just taking a little detour. Or maybe it was the other way around—maybe this path was the main road after all. With a man like McCarthy who'd antagonized people right and left, singling out the killer was hard. Yet for Caroline's sake, I hoped this person was an old enemy instead of a new one.

The computers were up when I walked into the library reference room the next morning, but a homeless woman sat hunched in front of the one machine with CD-Rom access to back issues of the *Boston Globe*, her face inches from the screen's yellow-lettered instructions. "Excuse me," I ventured.

She turned around. Shiny white theatrical makeup coated her face; bright orange hair stuck out, Medusa-like, from her head. Even though I'd noticed this woman before in the neighborhood, seeing her up close was a shock. I recoiled, then almost instantly felt guilty. She deserved my sympathy, not my horror. The reference librarian—a different one from the person who'd scolded me last night—stepped into the breach. "I found that volume of the *Britannica* you were asking about the other day, Mary. Would you like to take a look?"

The woman rose and followed the librarian. I slid gratefully into the seat she'd vacated and inserted the CD-Rom with the *Boston Globe* for the past six years. I could only search one year at a time. Where to start? The shooting must've occurred shortly before McCarthy had left BPD. But when was that? I decided to try two years back, typed in Ray McCarthy's name, and got several citations, but not to Ray McCarthy the cop. Three years back. The same thing happened. Four years back. Again the citations were for the wrong Ray McCarthys. "Quit holding out on me," I muttered. "It's got to be in here somewhere."

I tried five years back. Bingo! I could barely contain my excitement as citations flashed on the screen. I accessed the first story and read. My stomach clenched. No wonder Sergeant Rooney hadn't wanted to tell me the story. Or that family and friends of the dead boy had called for an investigation into police brutality and staged an anti-police demonstration. One news story stated:

> Angry demonstrators, protesting the slaying of fourteen-year-old Hugh Wilson by Boston Police Officer Ray McCarthy, as Wilson fled the scene of an alleged robbery at a convenience store in East Boston, thronged the steps of City Hall yesterday. Among them was Lance Littleton, 13, a Wampanoag Indian and close friend of Wilson's. Littleton waved a placard calling Sergeant McCarthy a murderer.

Murderer. The word leaped from the screen. Could Lance Littleton and the Indian at the village with the sign be the same person? No pictures accompanied the CD-Rom story. I needed the *Globe* on microfilm and this library didn't have it. Leaving the CD-Rom in the computer, I hurried from the building and headed for Harvard Yard.

22

"It was a fearful sight to see them thus frying in the fire and the streams of blood quenching the same, and horrible was the stink and scent thereof; but the victory seemed a sweet sacrifice, and they gave the praise thereof to God, who had wrought so wonderfully for them...." *Of Plymouth Plantation*

Martin paced beside his luggage, scowling at his watch, then at the roadway when I pulled up to the curb. No wonder: I was forty-five minutes late.

"I should've known better. It would've been faster to take a cab." He tossed his bag onto the back seat and got in.

"Sorry, there was an accident in the tunnel," I fibbed. The truth was that when I should've been on my way to Logan, I was still holed up in the basement of Harvard's Lamont Library, waiting to use the microfilm machine with a photocopier. "Hope you had a good flight, though."

Martin shook his head. "We hit bad turbulence an hour out of L.A. And the pilot was a woman."

In the interests of familial harmony, I let that one go. Martin told me to watch out for a cab, then a bus. Then he opened his laptop and was soon absorbed in a document. He reminded me of myself. We were both driven when it came to work. I'd be doing the same in his place, except that I couldn't read more than a few words without getting carsick.

Martin and our father were the only ones capable of

reading in the car and since our father had usually done the driving on the family trips of my childhood, Martin had relieved the monotony of those seemingly endless journeys. He'd been our talking book for *Wind in the Willows, Black Beauty, Treasure Island.* Martin's voice, high-pitched and eager, was inseparable from those stories.

Now, though, he was engrossed in his work in a way that had become almost impossible for me. "Eileen and Caroline will be certainly be glad to see you," I remarked.

"Mmmm." Martin didn't look up from the screen.

"Eileen especially. It's been tough on her, first with Caroline, then me."

"I wish she could've held it together for one more day. She knows I've got this big case pending. But where Caroline's concerned, she loses all sense of proportion. Makes me wonder sometimes why I married her in the first place."

I stared at Martin in disbelief. Looking straight at the computer screen, he displayed the finely chiseled profile I envied. My own features were more rough-hewn. We'd both gotten Dumbo ears, but while I hid mine behind a cloud of hair, Martin's baldness made his prominent.

"Pris wouldn't have carried on like Eileen," he groused. "She was always so calm and in control. You know she's a vet now? Married to a thoracic surgeon. With two sons. One at Stanford, the other at Brown. Of course, when you let her mouse die, that was the end of it."

"I can't believe what I'm hearing!" I exploded. "You've been talking to Mother, haven't you?" Our mother truly believes the grass is greener on the other side of the fence, that the road not taken should have been. Like Lot's wife, she is forever looking back with regret—though salinization has yet to occur; at seventy-nine she's still a killer on the tennis court.

Martin glanced over his shoulder. "Get out of the left lane. The driver behind you is flashing his lights."

I pulled into the right lane. A beige Camry sped past.

"Why didn't you use your blinker?"

"Nobody else was coming."

"Still, it's a good practice."

"Stop criticizing my driving and listen. Somebody deposited a severed head in your daughter's basket. She's pretty shook up because she's afraid a person she cares about is responsible. Eileen's on the brink because her baby's hurting. And you sit there wallowing in what might have been when you could help me figure out who did this awful thing."

"Help *you?*" Martin looked at me incredulously.

I filled him in on what I'd learned so far, including the latest development. Martin's fingers drummed on the dashboard. "Pull over up ahead there," he ordered.

Thinking it was a call of nature, I expected Martin to get out. Instead he turned angrily on me. "You have no business telling me what to do. You're ten years younger. You still don't know how to drive. And as for thinking you can solve a murder based on some silly dream! You've always been high-strung, difficult. At least while you and Simon were together, he was a steadying influence. But now Mother's right to be concerned."

I was so furious I couldn't speak. Finally I said between clenched teeth, "We'll talk about this later. If I'm going to get us to Plymouth in one piece, you'd better shut up."

Rubber screeched on asphalt. I swung off the shoulder onto the highway. Martin white-knuckled the door handle. He cleared his throat a couple of times during the ride but was otherwise silent.

"Slow down, you're going way too fast." Nate Barnes held up a restraining hand. We were standing in the living room of his condominium at Old Colony Estates. The lights were down low. Melissa Etheridge crooned in the background. I'd suggested meeting at Wood's, but Nate said he'd already put his feet up and was keeping them up. I'd have to come to his place to talk.

I opened my mouth and tried again. Nate shook his head. "You're still not making any sense. You need to calm down. Follow me."

A king-size waterbed dominated the bedroom. So that was what he had in mind. If he thought I was going to hop into bed with him just because. . . .

"Ever try one of these?" Nate gestured at a Nordic Track machine. Along with weights, a stationary bike, stair machine, and other exercise equipment, the Nordic Track was crammed into a space around the humongous mattress. I stared dubiously at the machine. In my opinion, exercise machines were modern-day forms of torture.

"C'mon," Nate coaxed. "Great way to let off steam." Reluctantly I let him rig me up on the Nordic Track. My arms and legs flapped back and forth. Clackety-clack. Clackety-clack. I felt self-conscious, silly. A hamster on a treadmill. Spinning endlessly, getting nowhere. But then the motion took over. Heart, lungs, limbs began working as one. Half-closing my eyes, I imagined myself on a real track, speeding past snow-blanketed trees, leaving my brother, my whole family far behind. Alone, then not alone. In front of me a figure loomed. The masked man unmasked to reveal slanted eyes that were obsidian black. The glow suffusing me shone in his eyes and in the smile playing at his mouth. I wanted to reach rather than get past him. He was a goal, not an obstacle as he'd been the other day at the village. Good Lord, what was I doing here? The warmth I'd felt changed to a cold sweat. My movements became forced, mechanical.

"What's the matter?" Nate demanded.

"What'd you do after I saw you at Plimoth Plantation Monday evening?"

"Dropped off the deer parts, drove home, showered and—" His eyes narrowed. "Why d' you want to know?"

"Just curious."

I tried to sound casual but Nate was onto me. He clamped a foot on the Nordic Track, bringing it to a halt. "Something's up. Come clean."

"I was attacked on Duxbury Beach that night."

"You think I—Jesus, you're one wiggy woman! After my shower, I picked up my kid at his mom's and took him out for pizza. I'll give you the number and you can check it out. Phone's over there."

My cheeks blazed with shame. "I'm sorry. Whoever attacked me could have followed me to the beach. You were the last person I saw before I left the village."

"That's why you came here tonight?"

"No. The demonstrator with the sign about Myles Standish—I think I know who he is."

"Looks like the same guy." Nate examined the photocopy I handed him with Lance Littleton's picture on it. We moved back to the living room and sat across from one another on leather chairs the color of lichen. "But I don't know of any Littletons in the Wampanoag community around here and I know just about everyone. It's not a big community."

"Maybe they moved away."

"Could be, but. . . ." He became thoughtful, then smacked his forehead with his fist. "I did know an Irene Littleton on Martha's Vineyard." He picked up a red clay pot from the coffee table and ran his fingers along its rounded contours in a sensual way.

An old flame. What did I expect? There had probably been plenty. Sans the sinister sunglasses, he was an attractive man. In spite of myself, I felt a flicker of jealousy.

"But that was a long time ago," Nate continued. "Couldn't have been more than ten or eleven myself and she was a few years younger. Visiting her grandparents for the summer. We used to play together on the beach. Had this powwow dress her grandmother made her. Even though we didn't have powwows back then."

"What happened to her?"

"Don't know. After her grandparents died, I never saw her again."

We fell silent. My promising lead looked like a dead end. "You're positive there are no more Littletons on the Vineyard or anywhere else around?"

"Positive. But it can't hurt to check the phone book."

We found plenty of Littles, several Littlejohns, a Littlefield, and a Littlehale, but no Littleton. "Maybe they don't have a phone or they've got an unlisted number," I said.

"Then how'll we find them?" Nate asked reasonably.

"There must be someone who knows what became of the family."

Nate rolled his eyes. "Persistent, aren't we?"

I bit my lip, half expecting another lecture on my shortcomings like the one Martin had delivered. Instead leather creaked. Nate rose with a sigh. "I'll make a few calls but I'm not promising anything." He disappeared into the bedroom, shutting the door behind him.

I glanced idly around. A beautifully woven rush basket perched on a tall, expensive-looking stereo speaker. A dream-catcher dangled over the desk above the notebook computer and laser printer. Artifacts and equipment. This was the fourth male preserve I'd invaded recently. Basile's was a bastion of impersonality, Conor's chockful of other people's things, but Seth Lowe's and Nate's each said something about the man who lived there.

A framed photograph on the bookshelf caught my eye. It showed a grinning, dark-eyed boy disguised as Batman. Nate's son. My gaze shifted to the books next to the photo. *The Soul of a New Machine, An Encyclopedia of Jazz, Where White Men Fear to Tread.* I slid out Russell Means's autobiography. The American Indian Movement leader glowered on the book jacket. Like Nate on the picket line at Plimoth Plantation and later on Caroline's doorstep.

I opened the book at random and scanned a page. Too dark to read. I found a dimmer switch. Light filled the room. I stared at the page again. Means described a plan to take white women as hostages, tape guns to their throats, and make a run for it. The lights went down. My throat went dry. Somebody playing *Gaslight?* Nate stood in the bedroom doorway, hands on jean-clad hips. "You've been messing with the switch." His tone was accusing. I felt like Goldilocks at the Three Bears' house. "There wasn't enough light."

Nate took the book from me and reshelved it. "A couple of people remember the grandparents and one also remembers Irene. But like I said: there aren't any Littletons on the Vineyard now."

"Isn't there someone else you can try?"

Nate flashed me an exasperated look. "There's one guy I'm still waiting to hear from. I left a message with his wife. But I doubt he'll know any more than the others."

I didn't try to hide my disappointment. "In that case,

I might as well go home."

The phone rang. Nate vanished into the bedroom. Five minutes later, he returned, looking embarrassed. "Irene Littleton moved back to the Vineyard several months ago. Lives in a trailer on property that belongs to weekenders from Boston. Looks after things for them in exchange for her rent."

"Great! Let's call and see if she's got a relative named Lance."

"She doesn't have a phone. The only way to reach her is to leave a message on the answering machine at the main house."

Nate's friend had told him the name of the Boston couple. We got the number and left a message. "Who knows if and when she'll call back," Nate said.

"Maybe we should just go out there."

Nate shook his head. "Too late tonight and I've got plans tomorrow."

"For Thanksgiving?" I asked without thinking.

"Thanksgiving!" Nate spat out the word. "We kept you whites from starving and you turned around and slaughtered us."

"That wasn't quite how it happened," I protested.

"No?" Nate shot back. "Ever hear of Metacomet?"

I shook my head.

"Obviously you haven't been to the exhibit."

"What exhibit?"

"*Irreconcilable Differences* over at the Visitor Center."

"I've been meaning to but—" I broke off, flustered as a kid caught unprepared for an exam.

"Well, when you do get around to visiting the exhibit, you'll learn all about Metacomet, or King Philip, as your people referred to him."

King Philip, yes, that name was familiar. My textbook writer's brain retrieved a boldface heading. "As in King Philip's War?"

"That's what your people call it. To us it was a war of ethnic cleansing. King Philip, a.k.a. Metacomet, was the Wampanoag sachem Massasoit's youngest son. Massasoit befriended the Pilgrims when they first landed. He thought they could live in peace. But by Metacomet's time, the Pilgrims showed their true colors. They told Metacomet he couldn't sell his own land without their approval. Then they executed three Wampanoag for supposedly murdering another. Metacomet had to go to war. His honor was at stake."

"I didn't know," I began.

"Of course not. This stuff doesn't get into the history books. They cry massacre whenever a white person is killed but don't mention that nearly a quarter of the region's native peoples were wiped out during King Philip's War. The survivors, including Metacomet's wife and ten-year-old son, were sold as slaves."

"What happened to Metacomet?"

"Betrayed by one of his men, ambushed, and shot. They brought his head back and displayed it at Plymouth."

So Wituwamot's wasn't the only skull stuck on the palisade walls. A tremor passed through me as I thought of Metacomet but also of McCarthy.

"Understand why I won't be eating turkey tomorrow?"

"What are you going to do?"

"Really want to know?"

Nate's tone and stance—shoulders squared, rocking forward on the balls of his feet—conveyed a mix of menace and mockery I found maddening. But I wasn't letting him get the better of me. "Yeah."

He gave me a long, measuring look. "Meet me at Cole's Hill tomorrow at noon."

"Why?"

"Just be there."

23

"Our harvest being gotten in, our governor sent four men on fowling, that so we might after a special manner rejoice together after we had gathered the fruit of our labors." *Mourt's Relation*

Gray light glanced off Nate's reflector glasses. I didn't need to see his eyes. From the tight line of his mouth I could tell his mood matched the gloomy weather. We stood on Cole's Hill overlooking Plymouth Harbor in a crowd of more than a hundred Native Americans. The National Wax Museum and the giant marble sarcophagus memorializing the fifty-odd *Mayflower* passengers—more than half of the original group—who had died during the first year loomed behind us. These were standard stops on the sightseeing circuit. But not now. Below, tourists milled around the absurdly inappropriate Grecian temple housing Plymouth Rock and streamed onto the *Mayflower II*.

From a small park across the street, a bronze statue of Governor William Bradford gazed up the hill at the statue of Massasoit, grand sachem of the Wampanoag, and according to the inscription I'd read many times, "Preserver and Protector of the Pilgrims." Massasoit's gaze was fixed not on Bradford, but on the ocean beyond, the ocean that had brought the ship whose replica was now docked in the harbor. From a distance the *Mayflower II* looked ridiculously small. A toy ship tossed into the water by a heedless

child. Its flags waved jauntily in the breeze and its furled
sails gave it an air of purposefulness. To my people this tiny
ship betokened a brave beginning in a new land; to Nate's it
epitomized the beginning of the end. Our Thanksgiving was
their Day of Mourning.

The faces around me bore witness. Tears glistened in
the older people's eyes; even the children were sober and
quiet. "Oh Creator, Mother Earth, and ancestors, hear us,"
a woman with long gray hair intoned. "Give us strength to
go forward without forgetting whence we came. Now we
are scattered and few, but let us live in the hope we will all
be united again."

I coughed. Nate frowned. Except to greet people he
knew, he'd said nothing since we'd arrived. I wondered if
he'd forgotten I was there. Now he made me feel like a fidg-
ety four-year-old disturbing her neighbors at church.

I was restless all right. Time was running out.
Sunday the village would close for the season and the interpreters would go their separate ways, the murderer includ-
ed—if he was an interpreter. I wished I could've persuaded
Nate to travel to the Vineyard today. The Lance Littleton-
Ray McCarthy connection could turn out to be a dead end,
but at least we'd have eliminated it as a possibility.

My eyes met those of another fidgeter, a boy wearing
a sweatshirt with a picture of Mickey Mouse and the word
"Disneyworld"on it. He smiled shyly.

"And they talk about genocide in Bosnia," a male
voice growled behind us. "What about genocide right
here?" The boy's smile faded. His gaze dropped to the
ground.

"At least they can't pretend we don't exist anymore,"
someone else declared. "Remember back in '70 when
Dennis Banks, Russell Means, and other AIM people seized
control of that little boat down there? They pulled up the
gangplank and tossed the dummies of Pilgrims overboard.
Would've torched the *Mayflower* if Dennis hadn't said no,
not with so many people on board."

"Wish they had set it on fire," another man said.

"Yeah," Nate agreed.

Set it on fire, set it on fire. The words echoed in my

brain. A shiver went through me. Suddenly I was back at a Black Panther rally in Oakland with Pat. "Gotta get a gun!" the Panther on the podium shouted and soon everyone, including Pat, was chanting, "Gotta get a gun! Gotta get a gun!" Everyone but me. The one outsider at that orgy of verbal violence, I'd never felt so out of place. Until now.

I glanced at Nate. His attention was elsewhere. Now was the time to sneak off. I took a tentative step. Nate didn't notice. Another step. Still no reaction from Nate. My eyes raked the crowd, looking for openings, measuring the distance to its outermost limits. It was hardly a static mass. New people were arriving all the time, making the throng both larger and more densely packed.

Another moment and I might have missed him moving along the fringes of the crowd. I recognized him because of his distinctive hairstyle, close-shaven around the sides and arranged in two braids on top. I craned my neck to be sure. Then I scooted back to Nate, bumping into him in my excitement. "The guy over there—it's Littleton!"

Reflector sunglasses jerked around. "Yeah. Let's get to him." Nate began a crablike maneuver. Facing forward, he edged sideways, going slowly and stopping often so as not to attract attention. I followed as best I could. Sometimes I lost sight of Littleton and thought he'd slipped away. Then someone in the crowd would move and he came back into view. Sentinel-like, he stood at the far end of the crowd, glancing nervously around.

"Watch it!" a voice bellowed. I froze. A man with an even higher Body Mass Index than Nate glared at me. Nate's head swiveled in our direction. "Sorry." I made a placating gesture. The man whose foot I'd trod on grunted and stepped back. Littleton was staring at the harbor.

Nate and I continued our painstaking progress. When Nate was within spitting distance of Littleton, a baby in a car seat carrier cried. Heads turned. The mother knelt and fumbled with the strap. The baby went on screaming. Nate stooped to help the woman. When they both stood up again, the mother had the baby at her breast. She beamed her thanks. Nate's smile died on his lips. Littleton was looking straight at him. He started backing away.

"Hey, man, it's cool. Just want to have a little talk," Nate said. Littleton turned and bolted down the hill.

We took off after him, swerving crazily to avoid people on their way up. A cooler whacked my thigh. Wincing with pain, I stumbled after Nate. At the bottom of the hill Littleton veered onto the sidewalk of Water Street. My feet pounded the pavement, sending shock waves through my body. My heart and lungs strained. A stitch grew in my side. Nate's broad back bounced in front of me. For a man his size he was fast. And he was gaining on Littleton. Less than half a block now separated them.

Beyond Littleton, on the far side of the street, an engine roared to life. A green sedan pulled away from the curb and headed toward us. Littleton dashed into the street, waving his arms frantically to flag down the car. For a moment the driver looked as if he would stop. But then the car surged forward. Nate yelled a warning. Littleton just stood there, arms waving like a windmill. The car rammed him. I felt the impact like a kick in my gut. Littleton's body flipped into the air, arcing with acrobatic grace. But no net broke the fall. Littleton landed with a dull thud, another kick in my gut. Nate dove into the street. Tires screeched. Rubber burned. The car spun around, coming back—No!

I shut my eyes and bumped into something hard. Rough wood ground into my cheek. A splinter pierced my skin. Creosote filled my nostrils. The pavement around me shook. I opened my eyes. People were running past to join the knot of horror forming around Littleton.

I didn't see Nate. Tears blurred my vision. In the distance an ambulance siren wailed. I loosened my grip on the utility pole and swiped at my eyes. Nate wobbled toward me, face bruised, sunglasses askew, but alive.

I ran toward him. He caught me in his arms. I wasn't sure which of us was shaking more. Over Nate's shoulder I glimpsed the ambulance tearing down the street like a red-eyed monster. The flashing blue lights of a patrol car followed. The crowd parted to reveal Littleton's smashed body. I cried out. Nate pivoted me around. "Nothing we can do. Let's go."

"But shouldn't we stay and tell the police what happened?" I gestured toward the patrol car, which had come to a stop.

"No cops for me, thanks." Nate propelled me away.

In the Jeep I buckled my belt and braced myself as if the vehicle were about to blast off. It didn't move. The ignition was keyless. Nate stared straight ahead, fists balled in his lap. "Dammit!" He slammed a fist into the steering wheel. "If I'd been faster, got him before he ran into the street."

"Don't blame yourself."

"Can't help it. The bastard just plowed him down, turned around and ran over him again."

"I thought you'd been hit, too." I felt another kick in my gut as the scene replayed itself in my mind.

"I rolled away in time. Littleton didn't have a chance." Nate yanked his glasses from his face, brushed at brimming eyes. "You get a look at the driver?"

"It happened too fast."

"What about the plates?"

I shook my head.

"So we've got nothing."

"Not quite," I said. "There's Irene Littleton. If she's related to him, she might know something."

Nate was silent a long while. Finally he said, "Okay. We'll go back to my place, check the machine in case she's called, get you fixed up and head out there."

"Get me fixed up?"

"You've got a chunk of utility pole right there." His finger grazed my cheek.

Nate sounded as if he had it together, but it was a solid minute before he started the Jeep. Then he drove like someone who's had one too many, knows it, and compensates by driving extra slowly and carefully, leaving plenty of space between the Jeep and other cars, and stopping well short of the intersection at every light.

The fog had rolled in and a fine drizzle was coming down when we reached the ferry at Woods Hole. Nate parked and left the car to negotiate with the steamship authority people. Because of the holiday schedule, departures were less frequent and space had to have been reserved in advance. I watched him confer with one man, then another and another until the windshield misted over and he was little more than an indistinct shape. Finally he disappeared into the office.

Caroline, Eileen, and Martin were having their Victorian Thanksgiving dinner at the Plimoth Plantation Visitor Center now. They'd made the reservation months ago, and although Eileen wanted to go elsewhere, Martin insisted they stick to their original plan. Within the village itself, there would be no special observance of the holiday. The Pilgrims hadn't celebrated Thanksgiving as we know it; they'd simply held a harvest feast.

Meanwhile, Nate and I were embarked on what might be a fool's errand. But after what had happened, I couldn't do a Norman Rockwell number with my family. I'd gag on the first bite of turkey. I'd left a message that something important had come up and I couldn't join them.

A rat-a-tat-tat on the window brought me out of my reverie. Nate's broad face appeared in the space he wiped clear. "Got us on a coal boat leaving in half an hour. Like something to eat?"

"Just coffee."

Ten minutes later, Nate returned with two coffees, two hot dogs, and a double order of French fries. He ate the food quickly, without enthusiasm. Midway through his second hot dog, he said, "Hope Irene can help us. But at the same time, I wish to God we didn't have to do this—especially if she's related to the guy who was killed."

"I know."

A voice yelled for us to pull ahead. Nate drove up the ramp onto the coal boat, carefully maneuvering between two other cars. More cars pulled in behind, then the roar of the boat's engine rushed in to fill the silence that had fallen between us.

24

"At which time . . . we exercised our arms, many of the Indians coming amongst us, and among the rest their greatest king Massasoit, with some ninety men, whom for three days we entertained and feasted, and they went out and killed five deer, which they brought to the plantation and bestowed on our governor, and upon the captain and others." *Mourt's Relation*

"Shit, missed the driveway." Nate made a quick U-turn and drove back to a dirt road with a hand-painted sign that said Peaceable Kingdom.

"This is it?"

"Yeah. I remember this place. Used to be hippies here. Then one night somebody lit a joint and forgot to put it out. House burned down, two people were killed, and the rest moved away. That must be the weekend house the people from Boston built." He gestured toward a gray saltbox on the left. Its windows were ablaze with light.

We continued down the road. Low bushes grew on either side and every now and then the shape of an abandoned appliance or vehicle rose like a ghost from the gloom. Irene Littleton's trailer was painted turquoise and rested on shocking pink cinder blocks. No lights were on, but Nate got out and knocked anyway. When he returned to the car, he said, "Let's go back to the saltbox. Maybe they'll know where she is."

I went to the door with him. It was opened by a

short, gray-haired man who resembled an overstuffed sausage. He wore a red apron with the slogan, "If you can't stand the heat, get out of the kitchen." His face glowed from that heat and the effects of the glass of red wine he held. The aroma of roast turkey filled the air. Suddenly I was hungry. All I'd eaten today was a stale corn muffin picked up at a convenience store on the way to Cole's Hill.

"Mr. Edelman?" Nate asked.

"What can I do for you?"

"We're looking for Irene Littleton."

"She's over in Edgartown waitressing. Drove her there myself several hours ago. She was going to take the day off so she and her brother could go to an Indian shindig on the mainland, but at the last minute she changed her mind."

"You mentioned a brother," Nate said. "Lance?"

"You know him?" Edelman inquired.

"Met him once." Nate's voice was flat, toneless. I wished we hadn't come.

For the benefit of those whose French was rusty or nonexistent, Le Poulet D'Or sported a golden hen over the entrance. Inside the decor was farmhouse French with a terra-cotta floor and long tables. Copper pots, garlic braids, and bunches of dried herbs hung from the ceiling. Despite the rustic appearance, a sign near the door informed patrons that a jacket and tie were required The prices probably weren't plebeian either. "I'm sorry," a sallow-faced maitre d' told us, "but we're closing early today because of Thanksgiving."

"We're not here to eat," Nate said. "We're looking for Irene Littleton."

The maitre d' scanned the nearly empty dining room, then directed us to a table where a woman in a short black skirt, white tuxedo shirt, and a black bow tie was collecting her tip.

"Irene?" Nate said.

She looked up, a striking woman with long black hair, dark eyes, high cheekbones, and a high-bridged nose.

"I left a message for you on the Edelman's machine. Nate Barnes, the, uh, voice from the past."

"Sure. Got your message and was gonna call but, hey, here you are." A smile lit up her face. "Nice to see you again, Natey. Or should I say Natey the Nuisance?" She punched his arm playfully.

Nate looked slightly embarrassed. "Nate'll do."

"Anyway, I am glad to see you. You live on the Vineyard?"

"No. Just here for a visit and figured I'd look you up." He grinned at her and she beamed back. I stood on the sidelines, feeling left out and even a little jealous. Nate and Irene Littleton had been childhood playmates so of course they were pleased to see each other, but in that pleasure lay the seeds of adult attraction.

I coughed. Irene noticed me. "Gonna introduce us?" she asked.

"Sorry. This is Miranda. A friend," he added with a trace of awkwardness. Irene and I shook hands. "If you don't have plans, maybe we could all go someplace for a drink?" Nate suggested.

"How about my place?" Irene offered. "It's not much, but it's home."

"Fine," Nate said.

He asked Irene to sit in the front of the Jeep with him. I slid into the back, again feeling like the odd person out.

"What brought you back to the Vineyard?" Nate asked once we were on the road. His tone was casual, but he drove the way he had after Littleton's death, slowly and carefully as if he didn't trust his reflexes.

"I was really happy here visiting my grandparents and I promised myself that one day I'd return."

"Don't blame you. Those were good times."

"Yeah. Remembering them helped me get through other times that weren't so good."

"Things haven't gone well for you?"

Irene sighed and said something in a low voice. I caught the words "ups and downs." "But hey," she continued, "I'm getting my act together. Got a roof over my head, work, and best of all, my kid brother and I are back together." Her upbeat manner made me like her and dread the prospect of bringing her down.

"Never knew you had a brother," Nate said.

"There's fifteen years between us. Lance wasn't even born when I was spending summers here. You'll probably meet him tonight, though. He went to the mainland for the day, but he'll be back."

I caught Nate's eye in the rearview mirror. *Tell her,* I pleaded silently. Nate frowned and shook his head.

"You and Lance should hit it off," Irene said. "You're a lot alike."

"How so?"

"You both have a knack for getting into trouble. When I think of some of the things you did."

"What about Lance?"

"That's a different story." A dark note crept into her voice. "Save it for another time." She was silent a moment, then brightening, she went on, "Remember when you and Jimmy Gibbs dressed up like pirates and nearly sank Grandpa's boat? He wanted your hides for that one. And then there was that other time."

Irene chattered happily on, oblivious to the bad news ahead. I wanted to scream, *Stop the car! Tell her the truth! I can't bear this charade any longer!* My skull ached with the strain of keeping silent. I shot Nate another imploring look in the rearview mirror, but again he shook his head.

Headlights illuminated a patch of the otherwise dark trailer. "That's odd," Irene said. "I thought Lance would be here."

My fingers dug into the seat cushion. Nate squared his shoulders. "Let's go in," he said.

Cinder block steps brought us into a room with a cracked green-and-gray linoleum floor that served as kitchen, dining room, and living room. The sitting area was furnished with a beat-up rattan love seat and rattan chairs with chartreuse vinyl cushions and pink piping. Someone's castoff porch furniture. The room was as cold as an unwinterized porch. I shivered and hugged myself.

"Sorry it's so cold," Irene apologized. "That was busted when I moved in and I haven't gotten it fixed." She pointed at a soot-blackened kerosene heater in one corner.

"I left a space heater on in the bedroom. I'd have one in here, too, but the wiring can't handle more than one heater at a time. Like a drink, something to eat?"

"No thanks. Why don't we sit down?" Nate said.

Wrapping a blanket around her, Irene curled up on the love seat. We sat opposite. "What is it?" she asked, noticing our long faces.

Nate took a deep breath. "Your brother showed up at a demonstration at Plimoth Plantation last Friday. I was there, but at the time I didn't know he was your brother. He waved a sign calling Myles Standish a murderer."

Irene looked surprised. "I didn't know he went to any demonstration. Was there a problem?" She sounded worried.

Nate nodded. "The actor who played Myles Standish was a former policeman named Ray McCarthy. Five years ago, McCarthy was involved in a brutal shooting. Your brother took part in a protest demonstration then, too. Do you remember that incident?"

"How could I ever forget!" Irene exclaimed bitterly. "The kid that cop shot was Lance's best friend. Lance was there when it happened. He saw Hugh die and it's haunted him ever since."

"Lance was at the convenience store with Hugh?" Nate queried.

"Yes," Irene replied slowly, eyes downcast. "He and Hugh were in it together. I know what they did was wrong, but Lance isn't a bad kid," she continued, "he's just had a hard time. Dad left after he was born, Mom went to pieces, and Lance and I wound up in foster care. We were with one family for awhile, but then they split us up. That's when Lance started getting into trouble. But all that's in the past. Why bring it up now?"

"The cop who shot Hugh was murdered last Friday," Nate said quietly.

Irene groaned and muttered something unintelligible.

"What?"

"The Wilsons. Hugh's family. Lance was in touch with them. But they—he—God, I wish he were here!"

Nate's face twisted with pain. "I'm awfully sorry,

Irene, but Lance is dead. He was struck by a car this after-noon."

"But that's not possible. He was just—" She stopped at Nate's solemn, confirmatory nod, seized her hair in two hunks, and screamed, "Noooo!" Still shrieking, she thrashed around on the seat, then shot up. The blanket fell from her shoulders, forming a dark puddle at her feet. She kicked it savagely aside, ran into the kitchen, flung open drawers, and rifled them.

Nate was behind her in a flash, grabbing her by the wrist and shaking hard. A carving knife clattered across the floor. I seized it, opened the door, and threw it into the bushes. Nate kneed Irene to the ground, pinning her arms behind her back. She struggled in his grip. "Let go!" She screamed something about needing to mourn in the old way.

"No!" Nate roared. "I'm not gonna let you hurt yourself."

Irene struggled a few moments longer, then her body went slack with defeat. Nate let go. She sobbed into his chest while he rocked her gently. I knelt beside them and stroked her hair.

Eventually we got her to lie down in the bedroom. Nate and I returned to the chilly main room. "That was awful," I said. "Why didn't you tell her straight out?"

Nate stared at me, appalled. "Would you walk up to someone you hadn't seen in years and say, 'oh, by the way, your brother was killed'? I wanted her to know me for a friend before I broke the news."

Chastened, I said nothing more. From the bedroom came muffled sobs punctuated by intervals of silence. Then it was quiet except for the low rumble of the space heater. The vinyl cushion of Nate's chair creaked as he shifted. "Looks like we're gonna be spending the night."

I surveyed the room doubtfully. The chairs were only suitable for slumber in an upright position. If Nate or I curled our long frames on the love seat, we'd be corkscrews by morning. "We can take the cushions and put them on the floor," Nate suggested. Seeing my hesitation, he added, "What's the matter? Never slept on a mattress on the floor?"

I'd done so all right. And not just slept—made love,

too. But that had been in another life. "Yeah but—"

"I'm not making any moves on you if that's got you worried," Nate said. "You can have your own mattress and put it wherever you like."

While Nate went to get another blanket from the Jeep, I arranged the makeshift twin beds. "I'm starving," Nate said when he returned. "How about a late-night snack? Or do you just want coffee?" Amusement flickered in his black eyes.

I was so famished I could've gnawed the rattan legs off the furniture. "I wouldn't mind a bite."

"See what I can find."

The tiny refrigerator and cupboards produced a half loaf of bread and a tin of something.

"Tuna fish?" I asked hopefully.

"Spam." Nate smacked his lips.

I made a face.

"It's not so bad heated up."

Nate was right. I ate a whole Spam sandwich, plus two pieces of bread fried in Spam fat, washing it all down with brandy from a flask Nate kept in his car.

"Hey, save some for me." Nate reached for the flask, tipped his head back, and drank. Beads of moisture glistened on his chin. He wiped them away. "Happy Thanksgiving, Miranda."

25

"... some of our people, impatient of delay, desired for our better furtherance to travel by land into the country, which was not without appearance of danger...." *Mourt's Relation*

A green sign with a Pilgrim stovepipe hat flashed past. Nate and I were on the road again, heading west on the Massachusetts Turnpike. Traffic on the Friday after Thanksgiving was light. We could be thankful for that and for Mr. Wilson's unusual first name, Jeremiah, which had made him easy to find in the phone book. Now if we could only reach a live person and know we weren't speeding across the state for nothing.

This morning Irene told us Mrs. Wilson had left a message for Lance on the Edelmans' machine. Mrs. Wilson said it was good to hear from him and that she hoped they could meet soon. Irene didn't know if Lance and the Wilsons had ever met. With her various jobs, she hadn't been able to keep close tabs on her brother. But she did know the Wilsons now lived in western Massachusetts because of the 413 area code on the number Mrs. Wilson had left.

Another sign—this one for a rest stop. I glanced at Nate, inscrutable behind his mirrored glasses. "Want to try the Wilsons again?"

"At the next stop."

"Why wait?" I asked.

"I want Italian and that stop's got a Sbarro. From then on, it's strictly Burger King and Roy Rogers."

"Your appetite knows no bounds."

"Look who's talking. You made short work of that Spam sandwich last night," Nate teased.

Last night. In spite of myself, I felt a twinge of tenderness toward him and not because of any sandwich. I'd lain awake, feeling the frigid air seep through the trailer's thin flooring and through the cracks in its louvered windows, listening to Irene's muffled sobs, Nate's snores. Remembering Lance Littleton's violent death and imagining Hugh Wilson's.

At some point toward the end of that long night, I heard Nate get up, use the bathroom, and come back into the room. I felt him standing over me. To my surprise, he covered me with his jacket. When he'd crawled back in his own makeshift bed, I pulled the jacket over my face. The heavy wool was rough against my skin, the smell of its wearer strong and male. I drifted off to sleep.

Twenty minutes later, irritation replaced tenderness. Nate strode across the Sbarro parking lot toward the Jeep, balancing a leaning tower of two styrofoam cups topped by a cardboard pizza box while wagging a thumb like a harebrained hitchhiker. It was a few moments before I realized he was giving me a thumbs-up sign.

"You reached the Wilsons?"

"Yup. We're dropping off a rug at their house around four."

"What?"

"Wilson has a carpet-cleaning business. He thought that's what I was calling about."

I rolled my eyes. "He's in for a surprise."

Forested slopes crowded in on the highway. By the standards of the West, where I'd grown up, these were mere hills. Yet they had constituted a formidable obstacle to settlers pushing westward. A superhighway breached the Berkshire Barrier now, but it existed, nonetheless, as both a physical fact and mental construct, making this westernmost part of the state seem a hinterland still. I understood why the

Wilsons had moved here. Like the Pilgrims who had sailed across the Atlantic, and the millions of emigrants who had inched across the continent, the Wilsons had wanted a place where they could escape a difficult past, make a new beginning. Whether they'd succeeded was another question.

We got off the Pike at Lee. Unlike its chichi neighbors, Lenox, Stockbridge, Great Barrington even, the town was plain and unpretentious, home to the working class rather than the wealthy. We stopped at a coffee shop to get directions to the Wilsons'.

They lived on a hill just up from the town center. The house was a white Cape built over a garage with a large red door. The garage and a paved parking area faced the street. Rugs of various sizes and colors were spread out on the blacktop and along a grassy strip of yard.

Inside the garage, a tall, gaunt man dressed in coveralls stared doubtfully at a rug with a geometric pattern and bright, bold colors at his feet. Stacks of rolled-up carpets lined the garage walls. In front of them were several rug-cleaning machines.

"Mr. Wilson?" Nate said.

The gaunt man glanced up at us, nodded, then returned to his study of the rug. "Let their tom spray this for close to ten years and now they expect me to get rid of the stink. Told them I'd do the best I can, but get a whiff of this."

I did; he was right.

"Got pet stains on yours, too?" Wilson asked.

Nate shook his head.

"No pets?"

"No carpet," Nate replied.

"Then why're you here?" Wilson demanded.

"It's about Lance Littleton. You and your wife were in touch with him, right?" I said quickly.

"What if we were? Who are you, anyway?" Wilson eyed us suspiciously.

"Private investigators," I said. Nate looked startled. Wilson frowned. I hurried on, hoping if I talked fast enough he wouldn't ask to see our licenses. "Lance Littleton was killed yesterday."

"What!" Wilson's surprise appeared genuine.

"He was struck by a car. The police are treating it as a hit-and-run, but Littleton's sister suspects foul play. She hired us to look into his death."

"Foul play, eh?" Wilson shook his head. "You're wasting your time. I don't know anything about that. Helen either."

"Helen's your wife?" I asked.

Wilson nodded.

"Is she at home?"

"No. She's in Syracuse with her sister's family and won't be home till Sunday. Only reason I'm here is I'm behind in my work and decided to come back early. Now if you'll excuse me, I've got to get my rugs in for the night."

Outside, the light was nearly gone and frost was in the air. Wilson walked to the edge of an Oriental and started rolling it up. Without being asked, Nate went to work on the opposite end. "When did you last see Lance?" Nate asked in a conversational tone.

Wilson didn't reply. Either he hadn't heard or had decided not to answer. Finally he said, "Five years ago."

"Not since?"

"No."

"But you were planning to meet?" I chimed in.

"We talked about it."

"But?" I prodded.

Wilson stopped rolling. "You got kids?"

"No, but—"

"I have a son," Nate intervened, "and I know how I'd feel if anything happened to him. Were you reluctant to meet because you were afraid it'd be too painful?"

Wilson nodded. "The phone calls from Lance were hard enough. Helen'd be upset for days afterward."

"Did he call often?" I asked.

"Always on the anniversary of Hugh's death."

"When's that?" Nate probed.

"November 22."

Nate and I exchanged glances. Wilson resumed rolling. "Lance also called whenever he was feeling especially down. Poor kid had a bad case of survivor's guilt.

Let's get this in."

Wilson and Nate hoisted the rolled-up rug and started for the garage. I put a hand under the sagging middle. "What did you talk about with Lance?"

Wilson waited until we were inside the garage before replying, "Helen was the one who talked with him. Let's put this down here."

Outside again, I seized the corner of a large dhurrie. The cotton felt cold and stiff to the touch. Rigor setting in. Wilson picked up the other end. Nate busied himself with the smaller rugs.

"What did your wife and Lance talk about?" I asked.

"Hugh and the past. Mostly she urged him to put it behind him. Get on with his life. Same as us. Moved here, had a child of our own."

Startled, I dropped my end of the dhurrie. "Hugh wasn't your son?"

"No. Helen's by her first husband." Wilson went on rolling and the bundled rug came out lopsided.

I frowned at the fat, messy end, pondering Wilson's words. "Hugh's biological father—does he live in the Boston area?"

Wilson gazed at the fat end of the bundle, too. "No. Moved to Florida right after he and Helen split up."

"Did you ever meet him?"

Wilson shook his head.

"Didn't he come to the funeral?" Nate asked incredulously.

"No. Howard was too broken up to come," Wilson said, looking at Nate. I looked at him, too, blowing on my red chapped hands to warm them.

"Really? I'm a divorced dad myself, but I can't imagine not coming to my own son's funeral."

"Your ex got custody?" Wilson asked.

"Joint," Nate replied.

"Howard fought for full custody and when he didn't get it he was furious."

"Howard's his first name?" I asked.

"Last. First name's Ben. Like I was saying, Howard was so furious about the custody arrangement he wouldn't have anything to do with Helen. Just sent a plane ticket when it was Hugh's time to visit. He doted on that boy, though. But who knows if he could've set Hugh straight."

"What do you mean?" Nate asked.

"Hugh was giving me and Helen a tough time. Just before he was killed, we'd arranged for him to live with Howard for a year."

Nate gave a low whistle. "No wonder Howard was broken up."

"That's putting it mildly," Wilson said. "He nearly went crazy with grief. Want me to take that side?" He pointed at the wide end of the rug.

"Thanks, I can manage," I said. We shouldered our ends and started for the garage. Nate followed with a rug slung over each shoulder. We marched into the garage, solemn as pallbearers with our separate burdens. After we'd deposited our rugs on the pile, Nate said, "Ray McCarthy, the cop who shot Hugh, was murdered a week ago."

Wilson's face was expressionless; he ground something underfoot. "Was he now?"

"Yes," I replied. "In Plymouth. He was working as an interpreter at Plimoth Plantation. Are you sure you didn't hear about it? It was all over the news."

"Maybe I did now that you mention it," Wilson conceded. "Just didn't make the connection between him and that cop."

"Do you think Lance was involved in McCarthy's murder?" Nate asked.

Wilson stared at the carpets stacked like corpses in a charnel house. Dust motes danced in the light from the overhead bulb. "How should I know?" He turned and stomped from the garage.

The only rug left outside was a white shag sprawled on the ground like the frozen body of a lamb. Wilson started for it, but Nate stepped in front of him. "I thought Lance might've told you what he was planning when he called last Friday."

"What makes you think he called then?" Wilson backed up toward the garage.

Nate advanced on him. "You said Lance always

called on November 22. Last Friday was November 22, the anniversary of Hugh's death and the day McCarthy was murdered."

Wilson's arm shot upward as if in salute. "Get out of here," he growled. Grasping the garage door handle, he pulled hard. The red door slammed down with a bang, obliterating him and his carpet mortuary.

26

"Upon which they saw there was no way but to take him by force.... But they found him to stand stiffly in his defense, having made fast his doors, armed his consorts, set divers dishes of powder and bullets ready on the table...." *Of Plymouth Plantation*

"Think Wilson had a hand in McCarthy's murder?" I asked as we pulled onto the Pike.

Nate looked thoughtful. "Dunno. But he sure as hell knows more than he let on."

"Right. Wish we'd questioned him more directly instead of getting sidetracked with that business about Hugh's biological father and the custody arrangements."

"My fault. I feel for the father, though. Poor guy thought he was going to get his kid back only to lose him for good."

"So where does this leave us?" I asked after a minute.

"With two bodies and a killer on the loose."

"There's still the outside chance Lance acted alone and that his own death was accidental."

"You don't seriously believe that, do you?"

"No. But I'd like to." It would have been so neat that way: McCarthy shot Hugh Wilson, Lance Littleton killed McCarthy, and his vengeful mission completed, died himself. Justice would have been done, the circle completed.

So neat, and so much better for Caroline if I could

have gone back to her and said, "Conor didn't kill McCarthy after all. Nor did any of your other new friends. It was someone entirely different. Someone with an older score to settle."

Instead I was left with the nagging sense that a piece was missing. It lodged itself in my brain like a splinter under the skin, stubbornly resisting the efforts of my probing needle to draw it out.

I was too tired to extract that piece now anyway. After the emotional high of locating Wilson, I was starting to crash, succumbing to the exhaustion that had been there all along. Exhaustion and an awful feeling of letdown. I glanced at Nate, wondering if he felt as discouraged as I did. Apparently not. His right hand was buried in a bag of Beer Nuts and his left pinky rested lightly on the steering wheel, as we sailed along at seventy-five miles an hour. Although it was now nighttime, he still had his sunglasses on. Irritated, I lashed out, "How dark does it have to get before you take those shades off?"

"Sorry." Nate took his hand out of the bag and removed the glasses. His brown-black eyes met mine. "Like me better this way?"

"Much."

"That's what Kathy, my ex, used to say." His tone was rueful. "Wish I could've obliged her more."

"Why couldn't you? Is something the matter with your eyes?"

"They're extremely light-sensitive."

"I'm sorry. Is it from illness or an hereditary condition?"

"My own doing."

"What?"

Nate sighed. "Back in the sixties I read a magazine article about stuff you could do to yourself to avoid the draft. I chose messing up my eyes with chemicals."

"Jesus, Nate."

"I know. But it kept me out of 'Nam."

So in his way Nate was a casualty of the Vietnam era. Like Conor? I still didn't know if he'd been involved in any of the violence that had occurred in the summer of 1970. But tomorrow I'd go to the library and find out. Saturday. There

wasn't much time left. On Sunday the village would close for
the season. The realization added to my gloomy state of
mind.

"You hungry?" Nate asked when we were almost to
Plymouth.

"Actually, I am."

"How about I fix us dinner?"

"Okay, but no Spam."

Nate chuckled. "This time it'll be something special."

That something turned out to be thick lamb chops
from Nate's freezer, which he defrosted in his microwave,
simmered in a sauce of red wine, currant jelly, and juniper
berries, and served with garlic-roasted potatoes and a
spinach salad.

"This is delicious," I said, helping myself to another
chop. "But it doesn't taste like any lamb I've ever had."

"It's venison from a deer I killed last fall."

I glanced from my plate to Nate and back again.
"That's right, you hunt. I'd forgotten."

"I thought they lynched hunters like me in your neck
of the woods," Nate said with a mischievous glint in his
eyes.

"You mean Cambridge? You might well be lynched
if you drove into town with a dead deer on your hood. Or at
the very least, somebody would approach you with an overly earnest expression and inform you that what you'd done
was wrong. Like someone did to me the other night."

"What did you do that was so bad? C'mon, tell
Uncle Natey."

"I thought it was Natey the Nuisance."

"Stop changing the subject and 'fess up."

I told him about the incident in the library.

Nate guffawed. "Just goes to show—"

"That I'm not the paragon you thought."

"No." He leaned forward, his expression serious.
"You're not a quitter. And that *is* admirable, Miranda."

I turned as red as the wine in my glass. "Flattery will
get you—"

"Nowhere," Nate finished. "Until you want it to."

He understood me too well. Squirming inwardly, I said, "No surprises, huh?"

Nate shrugged. "I wouldn't say that. One thing I really had wrong."

"Oh?"

"Had you pegged as anorexic, but you just polished off the two biggest chops."

I grinned. "My appetite's one of my best-kept secrets."

"Tell me about it." He grinned back.

Nate and I lingered over coffee and brandy. We'd been together more than twenty-four hours, shared some gut-wrenching experiences. I would feel strange without him. Finally I stood up. "I'd better be going."

"Not just yet." Nate rose and came over to me. We stood there, not touching, but occupying the same chunk of electrically charged air, so close I could smell him, see the rapid rise and fall of his chest, feel the warmth radiating from his body. Nate's lips parted in a slow smile that spread into his dark eyes. "Miranda," he murmured, ruffling my hair. Light as the brush of insect wings, his touch made me quiver deep within. His fingers drifted down across my cheek and over my lips in a gentle caress. I opened my mouth to taste their salty tang, but they had moved on to trace the jut of my jaw. "You have nice bones," he said, "and right here—" his index and middle fingers rested lightly on the ridge of my cheekbone— "you almost look Indian."

"Could be. The Lewis family was among the first set-tlers."

"Don't tell me they came over on the *Mayflower*?" Nate's tone was teasing, but there was something in his eyes that should've warned me.

"On the *Fortune* a year later."

"No kidding." The edge was in his voice as well as his eyes now. "So they were around when. . . ." His fingers pressed painfully into my cheekbone, then he withdrew them and turned away.

I stared at him, bewildered. "What's the matter?"

"Nothing. It's late and we're both tired."

I could've probed more, but what was the use? The moment of closeness had passed. Strangers again, we said good night stiffly.

I drove back to the playhouse, mad at Nate, then at myself. The mention of my ancestors had put him off, broken the spell. He probably figured they'd taken part in King Philip's War and other outrages committed against his people. But how absurd to blame me for things my family may have done three hundred years ago. As if anger, like hope, were a torch passed on from generation to generation. I hadn't experienced this kind of centuries-old animosity before and had trouble understanding it, though I was aware of its existence in other countries where certain groups seemed locked in a long-standing cycle of violence against one another.

Would I feel as Nate did if our positions were reversed and my people were the vanquished instead of the victors? Perhaps. But more to the point was the reality of his anger.

He'd spoken about King Philip's War as if it had happened yesterday. And knowing this was a sore subject for him, why had I mentioned my ancestors at all? I could have held off until we knew each other better, were less prickly and uncertain. Instead I had—deliberately?—thrown up a road block, halting the slow but steady advance toward intimacy. Nate was right about nothing happening between us until I wanted it to. He'd sensed my reluctance, fear even, but did he understand the tug of war raging inside me—how part of me wanted to speed back to his place, bang on the door, and beg for another chance?

At the thought of doing so, I was struck by a sickening sense of déjà vu. Twenty years ago, I'd banged and begged at Pat Landis's door. I wouldn't humiliate myself like that again.

The light on Caroline's answering machine winked at me like a drowsy cat's eye. Nate? My heart leaped. At least one of us wasn't so stubbornly proud to admit his mistake. Grinning foolishly, I pressed the button. Martin's frantic voice filled the room. "Caroline's gone. Call us immediately."

He answered on the first ring. "Miranda, thank God! We're worried sick. Caroline's not with you, is she?"

"No."

"Then she's run away. Please help us find her before—" His voice broke.

"I think I know where she is. Sit tight till you hear from me."

This time I chose the road to the Point over the beach route. I hit the sand at a gallop but soon slowed to a trot. If I didn't pace myself, I'd get winded too fast. I'd also run a greater risk of falling into one of the road's many ruts. The last thing I needed was a broken ankle. But as I jogged along, keeping my eyes on the ground, my thoughts raced ahead.

Conor remained an enigma. I wanted desperately to believe he wouldn't harm Caroline, but I couldn't be sure. If he were indeed the killer and Caroline voiced her, or rather my, suspicions to him, there was no telling what he might do.

On the other hand, I had no definite proof of anything about Conor. All I had was a string of suppositions, starting with McCarthy's original warning to "beware the drowned man whom it pleas'd the Lord to raise from his watr'y bier."

The drowned man resurrected—the epithet continued to bother me. I turned it over once again in my mind and suddenly I felt as if the scales were torn from my eyes: I understood the phrase's hidden meaning. The drowned man resurrected was both Master John Howland and Conor Day. Conor Day was the name of someone who'd drowned and whose identity the actor had assumed when he became a fugitive. That was why St. Etienne had no record of Conor Day. When he'd attended the college, he'd been someone else. Ice water shot up my spine. Dear God! Who was this man that Caroline had fled to?

I approached the house cautiously. Light shone behind a curtained window that was parted just enough to afford a glimpse into the living room. I saw no one, heard nothing except the hum of a nearby generator. I tried the door. Open.

I slipped inside. The aviary was there, but the only signs of human presence were two wine glasses and an empty bottle of chardonnay. I peeked into the bedroom. An open suitcase, filled with Conor's things, straddled the bed. They must be planning to flee, but where on earth were they now?

I hurried outside. A Blazer was parked in the rear so they had to be on foot. Perhaps they'd gone for a walk on the beach, yet I hadn't noticed anyone as I'd jogged up the road. I glanced around. The other houses on the Point were dark. Not so the lighthouse, a beacon to mariners—and star-crossed lovers, too?

Gurnet Light reared rocketlike from a grassy hillock in the midst of a level area enclosed by a split-beam fence. A sign warned visitors to stay within the enclosure because of possible cliff erosion. Conor and Caroline better have enough sense to heed it. I didn't see them in the enclosure, but maybe they were on the other side of the lighthouse. I took the steep, stone steps two at a time. Another warning— this one to stay at least fifty feet away because an extremely loud noise might sound unexpectedly. Not the best place for a tryst. And not one they'd chosen, I decided after circling the lighthouse.

Still, they might be over by the bunkerlike concrete structure with a horn squatting on its own mound behind the lighthouse. I raced to it. There were no steps so I scrambled up.

The far side of the bunker faced the sea. Outside the enclosure at the very edge of the cliff, a figure perched like a great bird poised for flight. The figure swayed slightly. Conor doing a reprise of John Howland on the storm-rocked ship's deck? But if he'd had a partner for his demonic cliff-side tango, she was gone. Had he let go of the rope and catapulted her into the abyss—a drowned woman with no hope of resurrection?

Terror tore at my insides. I avalanched down the mound to the fence and hurled myself over. "Where is she?"

"Gone," Conor said in a hollow voice, turning to face me.

"Where? If you've hurt her, I'll—" I shook a fist at him.

"She's not here. I sent her away. Look for yourself." He motioned me to come closer to the edge.

I held my ground. "I'm not playing that game again."

"You really think I'd harm her?" His foot slipped on loose dirt and he lost his balance, arms flailing the air, pea coat flapping around him. I caught him by the coattails and yanked hard. He staggered backward. I let go and we both plopped down hard. An instant later, I was on my feet again. "Where is she?"

"Beryl's," he panted.

"Beryl's?" Not trusting him, I took a few steps forward and peered down. Waves crashed against the rocks below. Caroline's body wasn't there. Relief flooded me. I turned back to Conor. "Get up. We'll go back to the house and call Beryl. Then the police if you're lying."

Conor punched in the number and handed me the phone. After three rings Beryl answered.

"It's Miranda. Is Caroline there?"

"Upstairs lying down," Beryl replied in hushed tones.

"Don't let her leave. I'll be there as soon as I can."

I called Martin, told him I'd located Caroline, that she was safe, and I was on my way to get her. I turned to Conor. "Give me a lift to the parking lot."

The Blazer rolled down the hill from the house and lurched onto the sandy track. My seat belt was too loose and I was thrown against the door. I cinched the belt more tightly. Conor fought with the steering wheel until the tires found purchase and we bucked forward.

"Sure this baby's gonna make it?"

"Always has before. But the going can be rough."

Conor leaned forward, chest hunkered over the wheel, neck craned, squinting at the lumpy stretch ahead. I gripped the door handle. Even so, I was bounced around a lot. This trip could've been avoided and everyone saved a lot of trouble if Conor had handled things differently.

"Why didn't you make Caroline go back to her parents? They're scared to death."

"I couldn't," Conor replied without taking his eyes off the track.

"No? There's a code among fugitives that says you don't turn one another in?"

Conor hit the brakes. The Blazer fishtailed and came to a stop at a right angle to the road, its rear tires embedded in dune brush. *Now you've done it*, I thought. Conor cut the engine and leaned toward me like a snake ready to strike. "What did you just say?"

"Nothing." I lunged at the car door, but he caught my arm and hauled me back.

"You called me a fugitive—why?"

In the moonlight his face was pale and drawn. A drowned man with a bit of the sea in his left eye. Even if I escaped from the Blazer, I wouldn't get far before he caught up with me. My big mouth had gotten me into this mess; now it better get me out. "I don't know why I said that."

"Of course, you do. You've been asking questions about me and now it's my turn. Who's Pat?"

So Beryl had told him about my impulsive outburst at McCarthy's wake. "An ex-lover," I replied evenly, hoping against hope I could leave it at that.

Conor's grip tightened on my arm. "When was he your lover?"

"A long time ago."

"How long?"

"More than twenty years."

"And you think you saw me at his place?"

"I did for a moment, but then I realized how unlikely it was that you were the same person I glimpsed so long ago."

I expected him to agree with me. Instead his craggy features knotted into a frown. "Where was this?" His hand felt like a tourniquet pulled tight around my arm.

"What does it matter? I've already told you it's highly unlikely you're the person I saw then."

The tourniquet squeezed more tightly. "Where?"

I shook my head. "This is crazy."

"Maybe, but now you've got me wondering if we've met before. Let's see. More than twenty years ago, you were in college. At Stanford."

He was silent, tracking me through the dark house of memory as I'd tracked him. I held my breath, imagining him blundering through the many shadowy rooms, knocking over furniture, groping for the light. "Che," he said finally. "His real name was Pat, but we called him Che because that's who he looked like. Che was your lover. I hid out at his place after—"

"Don't!" I cut in. What I didn't know couldn't hurt me. And most of all, it couldn't hurt Caroline. I had a childish impulse to cover my ears. But there was no escape.

"You started this, Miranda," Conor said grimly, "and I'm going to finish it. When I stopped off at Che's, I was on the run from an act of violence in another state."

A word blazed like lightening through my brain. "It was the armory," I blurted. "The attack on the National Guard Armory in Ann Arbor—that's what McCarthy was hinting at with the story of how the Pilgrims besieged Morton and his men in their arsenal."

"I didn't kill him," Conor said simply.

"Who? The night watchman or McCarthy?"

"Neither of them. Do you believe me?"

I was tempted to lie and tell him what he wanted to hear, what was in my best interests to say. Instead I risked honesty. "I don't know. But right now my main concern is getting Caroline back to her parents. That's my only agenda for tonight. Can we go?"

"So you can head straight to the police? I'm not that stupid, Miranda."

I fought to wrench free of him, but he clung to me with a drowning person's desperate grip. Then abruptly he let go. My shoulder banged into the car door. I leaned heavily against the door, too stunned to open it.

"Maybe I don't care anymore," he said, turning the key in the ignition. He stepped on the gas. The front wheels spun in place. He put the Blazer in reverse and backed further into the dune brush. He tried to pull forward, but again the front wheels spun, digging in deeper. He backed up and repeated the maneuver, jockeying the car back and forth the way I'd been taught to do when trapped in snow. After several tries, he gave up and got out to examine the wheels.

When he returned, he said, "I've got some boards in the back that I'm going to put under the front tires. You steer while I push." He removed a couple of two-by-eights and positioned them under the front wheels. Then he disappeared behind the rear of the car. "Ready!" he yelled. I stepped on the gas. The tires cleared the boards but promptly got stuck again. Conor repositioned the boards and we tried again. This time the Blazer didn't stop.

Conor ran to the front of the car and jumped in beside me. I accelerated. The Blazer leaped forward and hit a bump, jouncing us so that our heads grazed the roof of the car. "Watch it!" Conor warned. "There's no big rush. Caroline's not going anywhere."

"How do you know?"

"Because she thinks I'm meeting her at Beryl's later tonight so we can run away together."

"What!"

"It was the only way I could get rid of her," Conor replied miserably. "She wanted us to leave immediately. Said she knew I was in some kind of trouble, but it didn't matter, she'd stand by me because she—she loved me so much." He shook his head and our eyes met in a moment of understanding: two forty-somethings appalled by the reckless folly of youth.

"I tried to reason with her," Conor continued, "but she wouldn't listen, just kept repeating that she loved me and nothing else mattered. Finally I persuaded her to wait for me at Beryl's while I took care of some business. I figured Beryl could talk some sense into her."

"And you'd sneak off without her?"

Conor threw up his hands. "What else could I do? The police are going to find out about the blackmail and my past eventually. I'd have left a lot sooner if it hadn't been for Beryl. She said running would look like an admission of guilt. But tonight I couldn't take it anymore. My bags were already packed when Caroline showed up."

"Why didn't you take off the minute she was gone?"

"I was going to, but have you any idea what it's like to always be watching your back? I went out to the cliff."

"Were you going to jump?"

"I don't know. Maybe." He buried his face in his hands, muffling his next words. "Hasn't been much of a life."

Minutes later, I pulled up beside my car in the beach parking lot. I was about to slide from the driver's seat when Conor put a hand on my arm, detaining me. Now what? I hoped he wasn't having second thoughts about letting me go.

"Tell Caroline I'm sorry."

27

"He and some of his had been often punished for miscarriages before, being one of the profanest families amongst them; they came from London, and I know not by what friends shuffled into their company." *Of Plymouth Plantation*

The downstairs lights were on at Beryl's, but when I rang the bell no one answered. Maybe Beryl had grown weary of waiting and dozed off in her chair. I rang again. Still no answer. After the fourth try, I went around to the back. A potted tomato plant lay on its side, dark soil staining the patio. I stepped around it, catching a whiff of the plant's pungent odor.

Somewhere close by, a baby wailed, its cries high-pitched and eerie like the coyote calls I'd heard as a child at night in suburban Southern California. It was neither a baby nor a coyote, but a cat in distress. I banged on the back door. No response. The knob turned. I pushed the door open. "Beryl?"

Silence. Then a scuffing sound and a flash of calico fur as Love dashed into the hall and up the stairs. From where I stood in the dining area, I had only a partial view of the living room—one end of the sheet-shrouded couch, part of an armchair with its stuffing leaking out, on the floor one blue-slippered foot.

My legs went leaden. It seemed to take hours to walk the short distance to where Beryl sprawled. Her eyes were wide and staring, her face no longer a weathered apple, but white and waxy, its pallor accentuated by the vivid scarlet surrounding it. Blood formed a band at Beryl's throat and billowed like a cape around her body. One fold of the bloody cape pointed toward the far wall. Wrestling lay crumpled below it. The cat must have attacked the killer, who then hurled it against the wall. The poor creature had died as it lived, defending its owner.

The room started spinning. I reached out to steady myself, groping through plant leaves until my fingers found a table's hard edge. I wanted to turn and run. Instead I stood rooted to the spot, unable to tear my eyes away from the two bodies.

Above I heard a noise. Caroline? My heart pitched against my rib cage. Was she still asleep, hiding, or. . . ? I refused to consider the last possibility. I had to get her out of here.

I started up the stairs. Love streaked past. Fleeing the killer still lurking in the house? I longed to escape myself. But the thought of Caroline cowering in a corner, immobilized by terror, propelled me forward.

The bedroom door was shut, the light off. I took a deep breath, steeling myself against what I might find. Then I flung open the door. It banged against the inside wall, swung back toward me, then was still. Too still. Was I too late? With trembling fingers I fumbled for the switch.

Prepared as I was for the worst, the utter ordinariness of the scene took me by surprise: covers turned back on the bed, an indentation in the pillow where Caroline's head had been, her lavender scrunchi on the nightstand. She might have just gotten up.

I felt suddenly giddy and light-headed. I picked up the scrunchi and pressed it to my face, breathing in the sweet herbal scent of her shampoo. Caroline. She was safe after all. I must've made a mistake. What I'd seen downstairs and what was here didn't belong together. These two rooms couldn't exist in the same house. One was real, the other a figment of my overwrought imagination. In a moment Caroline would walk through the door.

Metal creaked. The closet door knob turned.

"Caroline?" I grabbed the lamp from the nightstand, ripped the plug from the socket, and jumped to one side of the door. A hunched figure crept from the closet. I was about to bring the lamp crashing down on his head when he spun around and saw me. "Miranda! What the devil?"

"Don't come a step closer!" I brandished the lamp.

Seth Lowe's face twisted with horror. "You don't think I—I loved Beryl—more than my own life. I came here to warn her, but I was too late."

"Warn Beryl? Where's Caroline?"

"Caroline?"

"She was right there!" I gestured wildly at the bed.

Lowe stared at the turned-down covers. "Omigod, Nan couldn't have—"

"What?"

"We had a huge fight. I told Nan I loved Beryl and wanted a divorce. She screamed she'd kill Beryl first and ran from the house. I got here as soon as I could but—" He covered his face with his hands.

"Did you call the police?" I demanded.

"No. When I heard someone at the front door, I panicked. I ran up here and hid."

I reached for the phone on the nightstand. It rang before I could pick it up. My hand stopped in midair. Who could be calling now? Seth and I exchanged fearful glances. I cradled the receiver gingerly as if it were a live grenade. "Yes?"

"Miranda—Conor. Caroline just phoned. She was hysterical, said she had to leave Beryl's, but wouldn't say why. She asked me to meet her at the village. What in heaven's name is going on?"

I told him about Beryl. "God—No!" he cried. "Who could've done such a thing?"

"Seth's here. He thinks Nan killed Beryl in a fit of jealous rage. Caroline must've heard something, come downstairs, and found Beryl dead. Are you going to the village?"

"I told Caroline I would." He sounded defensive.

Sure, I thought. Just like you promised you'd meet her at Beryl's when you had no intention of doing so. "I'll meet you there. Where do I find Caroline?"

"She'll be waiting inside the Fort/Meetinghouse. She said she'd leave the northern flanker gate open."

I headed for the door. Seth grabbed my arm. "You can't just leave," he protested.

I shook him off. He stumbled backward into the bed and sat down. "But what about me? What am I going to do?" he moaned.

I felt a stab of pity. He looked so forlorn with his shoulders slumped, one hand tugging distractedly at his shock of graying hair. His present helplessness was a far cry from his calm take-charge attitude during last Saturday's crisis. Then he'd known what to do because he was William Bradford, governor of Plimoth Plantation. Now he was just an ordinary man trying to cope with a tragic loss. And the only advice I could spare was practical rather than existential. "Call the police."

Caroline's car wasn't in the staff parking area. Nor was Conor's. She could've parked elsewhere, though, and I didn't expect him yet—if he showed at all.

I ran down the hill toward the Carriage House Crafts Center, sneakers thudding on the pavement. A dog barked. I stopped in my tracks. A guard dog? The barking sounded distant, but I couldn't be sure. Kids often wander in after hours, Seth Lowe had said. But not this late at night. They'd be safely home in bed by now—where I'd be, too, if it weren't for Caroline. I'd fetch her, then beat it.

I crept the rest of the way down the hill. The Carriage House Crafts Center was dark and deserted. I felt vulnerable out in the open. I ducked into the woods, following the trail used by the interpreters. Dry leaves crackled underfoot. My toe landed on something soft and squishy. Suppressing a scream, I switched on the flashlight I'd brought from the car. A smashed jack o'lantern leered up at me. I hurried on, my flashlight trained on the ground to avoid other unpleasant surprises.

Moments later, I came out into the fields. Wizened cornstalks rustled in the wind. Beyond, the weathered timbers of the palisade gleamed like bleached bones in the

moonlight. Once real bones had perched atop these walls—
the skull of Wituwamot, then of Metacomet. A thrill of fear
shot through me.

At this time of night there was no rumble of traffic,
only the lap of waves against the shore at Plymouth Beach.
Long ago, one might've heard the slap of moccasins on the
Indian trail that was now Route 3A. I half imagined I could
hear them now. Ridiculous. My brain was playing tricks on
me—unless those soft footfalls belonged to Conor. Or
Caroline.

I glanced quickly around but saw no one. The
flanker gate yawned open ahead. Caroline was in there,
waiting for Conor. She'd have to settle for me, but maybe
now after all she'd been through tonight she would welcome
me with open arms.

I scurried through the gate. To my right a rounded
shape loomed. A scream caught in my throat. The next
instant I recognized the shape for what it was: the domed
oven where the Pilgrims baked their bread. In the moonlight
the village was spooky and unfamiliar.

Skirting the garden and the back of a dark, silent
house, I came into the main street and stopped dead. The
barrel of an enormous gun poked from behind a wooden
barricade, pointed right at me. I nearly threw up my hands
and begged whoever was hiding behind the redoubt not to
shoot. Then I saw the two other guns and reminded myself
that all three were part of the setup. *Murtherers*, the
Pilgrims had called these guns. Three hundred years ago,
they would have been used to clear the streets in times of
trouble. Now they were harmless props.

Still, to reassure myself, I approached the redoubt
and beamed my flashlight inside. An owl screeched. I
jumped. My flashlight clattered into the redoubt. Clumsy.
But with the moonlight I didn't need it.

The redoubt stood at the midpoint of the hill sloping
down toward the bay. From here the broad main street with
its huddle of houses on either side climbed to where the
Fort/Meetinghouse hulked like a dark, brooding castle with
its own gated enclosure.

Keeping to the middle of the street, I started up the

hill. On my left at ground level, the two windows of the Billington hovel stared blankly at me. The hovel's interior extended underground, but viewed from the outside, it resembled a torso severed at the—No! I pushed the gruesome image aside, but another image, equally gruesome, replaced it: Elinor Billington, a.k.a Beryl Richards, sprawled on the floor of her real-life home.

I fought back the horror of that vision and forced myself past the hovel, then the Allerton house. Two more houses on each side, followed by a stretch of livestock pens, and I'd be at the Fort/Meetinghouse gate. I could see the building's peaked roof and the upper story with its slitted windows through which cannon could be fired.

Caroline might be up there, watching from a window for Conor. "Caroline!" I called, waving my arms. No response. Maybe I was too far away. Or she was holed up in the cavernous first floor, empty except for a few benches and the railed-in pulpit.

The owl screeched again from somewhere ahead. Something rustled by the last house before the Fort/Meetinghouse. Conor or the security guard? But they wouldn't sneak around. They'd come out into the open. My heart pulsed wildly. I broke into a run.

A frantic screech and a sudden movement—the flapping of wings or a ghostly arm beckoning? I flew past the last house and the livestock pens, through the gate to the Fort/Meetinghouse, Caroline, and safety.

Inside, darkness enveloped me. "Caroline?" No answer—just the loud hammering of my heart. I took a step forward, crashed into a wooden barrel. My arms swung out, beating the air. Hands slammed me into a wall, pressing my face against rough boards. A flashlight blinded me.

"What the hell're you doing here? Where's Conor?" Basile thrust his bloodhound face into mine. He twisted my arm. "Where is he?"

"Where's Caroline?" I gasped.

"Over there." The beam of light cut through the darkness to where she lay hog-tied on the ground at the foot of the pulpit. Gray duct tape covered her mouth. But her eyes communicated her terror. "Caro—baby!" I wanted to go to her, assure her everything would be all right, that we'd get out of this somehow, but Basile was already tying my hands. Rope burned my wrists as he yanked me to my knees. I looked up at him stupidly. "You and Conor are in this together?"

"Yeah right," he said roughly. "I'm helping out by getting his next victims ready. Then after he's killed you two, he'll turn the gun on himself in a fit of remorse."

A deep chill passed through me, followed by a flush of anger. How could I have been so foolish as to blunder into a trap laid for Conor? I should've known better than to come here alone.

"Lie down!" Basile barked, jabbing my back with the heel of his hand.

I sprawled on my stomach, twisting my head toward Caroline, determined not to let her out of my sight. I kept my eyes trained on her dim shape until Basile squatted beside me, blocking my view. The rope was looped around my ankles now. He tied a knot, pulled it tight. My arms were jerked backward over my head, my feet left the ground. Muscles stretched to the snapping point. I groaned.

"The more you struggle, the worse it gets," Basile said. "Captain Standish tied up John Billington like this for a farthing o' an hour for refusing to take his turn at watch. But poor Billington never got a chance to pay the bastard back."

Billington and Standish—what was he talking about? Then it dawned on me. "You killed McCarthy! But why? I thought you were friends."

"I only chummed up with Ray to win his trust. But all along I was waiting to get my revenge. He murdered my son. Emptied a whole clip of ammo into the poor kid while he clung to that chain link fence for dear life."

Basile's face twitched with anguish as he spoke, then like a dying creature that's given up, it went still. The droop of his features seemed even more pronounced, as if his flesh, his very bones, had been dragged further into the well of his grief.

"You're Hugh's father?" I stared at him, dumbfounded. The next instant, the missing pieces clicked in: his reaction to the mock shooting, the snapshot he hadn't wanted me to see, the very part he'd chosen to play—John Billington, an angry, quarrelsome man with sons who were forever getting into trouble.

"Yes," he replied in a voice as bleak as his face. He looked awful, but I couldn't take my eyes from his ravaged features. I felt pulled into that bottomless pit along with him.

But the killing hadn't stopped with McCarthy. Pity switched to anger as I thought of his other victims. "What about Lance Littleton and Beryl Richards? Did they have to die, too?"

"That's enough!" Basile reached for the roll of duct tape. Caroline moaned. In a moment I'd be mute like her. I might never have a chance to ask the question that had nagged at me from the beginning.

"I guess I understand," I said, hoping to placate him and buy time. "They had to be silenced—Lance because he was your accomplice and Beryl because she figured out you were the killer. But why put McCarthy's head in Caroline's basket? What did she ever do to you?"

Basile twirled the roll of tape on his finger, enjoying keeping us in suspense. "Nothing," he said finally. "It was just convenient."

I couldn't believe my ears. All this time I'd been convinced McCarthy's murderer bore a grudge against Caroline. "But—"

The owl screeched sharply. Basile dropped the tape and grabbed his gun. "Goddamn bird!" he growled. There was a rustling noise. Basile flattened himself against the wall just inside the open doorway.

We waited, Basile with his gun cocked, ready to pounce on his next victim, Caroline and I trussed like hapless heifers. Seconds passed; they might have been hours. My arms and legs throbbed with pain. A ringing filled my ears as I strained to hear the telltale sound that would decide our fate.

What if Conor never showed? He'd spent most of his adult life on the run. Why should he behave differently now?

Because he had to; he was our only hope. But where was he? He should be here by now. Unless something had happened. I pictured him stuck on the road from Gurnet Point, the Blazer's wheels spinning helplessly. *Get yourself out,* I ordered silently. *Basile's not going to wait all night.*

How much time did we have? I tried vainly to recall whether the moon had been high or low in the sky. Basile would want to leave well before dawn. To stay any longer was taking too big a chance. If Conor didn't come soon. . . .

Shoes scuffed somewhere outside. Basile's shoulders knotted. Caroline's body rocked. Why? She couldn't escape. She must be trying to warn Conor. God, no! I shook my head. She ignored me. Her body hit the pulpit railing. Basile pointed the gun at her. For one heart-stopping moment, I thought he'd shoot. Instead he bounded across the room and jammed the barrel against her head. "Don't even think about it."

Basile scuttled back to his post by the door. His bones cracked as he rolled his neck. Conor must've gotten scared off. Maybe he'd gone for help. How much longer would Basile wait before—I swallowed hard.

"Shut up!" Basile mouthed furiously, aiming the gun at Caroline again.

I was afraid to breathe. My limbs were numb. My brain fogged. From faraway a voice called, "Caroline, are you there?" Basile frowned at Caroline.

"Caroline?" the voice, muffled and unfamiliar, called again.

Basile sniffed the air as if trying to pick up Conor's scent and gauge his whereabouts. Then he went over and squatted beside Caroline. He ripped the tape from her mouth.

"Are you in there?" the voice called.

Basile nodded at her. She said nothing. Basile poked her with the gun. "Answer him."

"Yes, Conor," she said in a quavery voice.

"Then come on out."

Basile glared at the entrance. Things weren't going according to plan. Conor was keeping his distance, playing it safe. Basile hesitated, then seemed to reach a decision. He untied the knots. Caroline's arms and legs flopped to the ground. She lay there, motionless.

"Coming, Caroline?"

Basile jerked her to her feet and shoved her toward the doorway. She wobbled past, so close that if my hands hadn't been tied I could've reached out and touched her ankle. Caroline. One false move and he'd gun her down. My neck shot out like a snapping turtle's. But before I could sink my teeth into the flesh of Basile's leg, he passed out of range.

Caroline stood in the doorway, Basile to one side, hidden by the shadows. Conor must see her, yet he made no move. Basile stabbed the gun into the small of her back. "Call to him, get him to come to you," he rasped. She was silent. "Do it!"

"Conor?" Her voice was faint and tremulous.

A cold sweat drenched me. Conor couldn't stall forever. He had to show himself. Then Caroline would run to him, run and crumple like paper as the bullet pierced her. I tugged violently on the rope. A searing pain ripped through my arms and legs. I'd only made things worse. But maybe not. Caroline's rocking gave me an idea. Basile was about four feet away. I gritted my teeth, steeled myself for the assault. Blood roared in my ears. I barely heard Conor say, "Over here."

Caroline swiveled toward the voice. Basile leaped from the shadows after her. "Watch out!" I shrieked, pinwheeling myself into his legs. He staggered forward. A whizzing sliced the air. Basile howled. His gun went off. Caroline screamed.

28

"There was a lusty man and no whit less valiant . . . stood behind a tree within half a musket shot of us, and there let his arrows fly at us." *Mourt's Relation*

Basile danced a wild jig above me, gasping with pain as he clutched at something stuck through his chest. He twisted at it like a key on a windup toy he was trying to turn off. I strained to see Caroline but couldn't find her. Behind Basile, someone came running. A fist sent him crashing to the ground. He whimpered and writhed slowly, clawing at the arrow in his chest. Now I saw Caroline sprawled in the dirt on the far side of the doorway. Let her be alive, I prayed. A shadowy figure crouched beside her. With help she rose unsteadily to her feet. I let out a huge sigh.

They both came to me—Caroline and—I blinked. My brain must be befuddled by pain. It wasn't Conor. Caroline stared wonderingly at him. "Who are you?"

"Nate!" I cried. He bent over me, working at the knots that bound me. The rope went slack. I lowered my arms, but my leg muscles were too kinked to move. Nate massaged each leg before straightening it and lowering it to the ground. "Better?"

"Much. How did you know to come here?"

"Irene found a piece of paper with an address and phone number among Lance's things. When I got there, this guy was just leaving with your niece at gunpoint. I followed them here. Then you showed up. Tried to get your attention but—"

"You were the owl?"

Nate looked sheepish. He started to nod, then his head jerked around. The whimpering had stopped. Basile was gone. Nate sprang to his feet. I struggled to rise, but Nate restrained me. "Stay here." He took off after Basile. Caroline watched Nate's retreating figure with terror in her eyes. "We'll get help," I said. "What happened to the security guard?"

"Out cold, but we can call the police from his office."

"Let's go." I scrambled to my feet but almost immediately felt dizzy.

"You okay?" Caroline extended a hand to steady me.

"I think so." I took a few uncertain steps, then felt something hard underfoot. Basile's gun. I grabbed it. Holding hands like schoolgirls, Caroline and I ran down the hill toward the flanker gate.

We were almost to the redoubt when we heard footsteps clattering on wood. We froze. Nate? Basile? Where?

"The Eel River Nature Walk," Caroline said.

"Isn't that gate locked?"

"Must've climbed the fence."

A blood-chilling cry shattered the stillness. Caroline's fingers crushed mine. We looked at each other, wanting to believe the cry had come from Basile. But if it hadn't? Basile was wounded but desperate.

"Call the police. I'm going after them."

"But—"

"Take this." I thrust the gun at her.

"What about you?"

"I've got my Swiss Army knife," I lied, sounding more courageous than I felt. "Go!"

Caroline raced toward the open gate. I sprinted in the opposite direction. A livestock pen extended almost the entire length of this side of the stockade. I clambered over the fence, stumbling on the uneven ground. Rounded shapes huddled at the far side of the pen. One peeled away and trotted toward me. A pig, or rather a bristle-coated boar. These animals had been specially back-bred to produce a wilder seventeenth-century variety.

I streaked toward the palisade with the boar mad in pursuit. I reached the fence, found a foothold, and hoisted myself up, straddling the jagged stakes at the top. Below, the boar reared on its hind legs. Teeth snapped the air, inches from my dangling sneaker. I swung my other leg over. So much for historical correctness. I'd settle for a tame anachronism over vicious authenticity any day.

At the start of the nature walk, wooden steps descended steeply to the boardwalk below. I careened down, nearly losing my balance before I hit bottom. Ahead, the boardwalk cut a pale swath between the marshlands of the Eel River estuary on the left and a jungle of holly and giant rhododendron bushes on the right. After about a hundred yards, the boardwalk curved into the woods and disappeared.

Someone could easily be lurking around the bend. I approached cautiously. Boards creaked underfoot. My heart rapped a staccato rhythm. Before me, a roof of tangled branches arched over the walk. The arbor provided a shady refuge in summer. Now the darkness made it dangerous.

At the entrance to the tunnel's black mouth, I stopped. *Don't go in there!* an inner voice warned. I forced my feet forward, arms outstretched, groping my way, blind and terrified.

Smack! Something hard slammed into my forehead. Sticks clawed at my eyes. Pushing the branch aside, I stumbled forward and nearly tripped over a sandbag. Not a sandbag, a body. Basile or Nate? In the darkness I couldn't tell. I sank to my knees. With palsied fingers I felt around, found a face, strands of silky hair matted with a sticky substance.

Nate. My heart dropped into my gut. I spoke his name. He groaned and shifted slightly. "Don't try to move," I said. "Caroline's gone for help. We'll get you to a hospital." I reached for his hand, but he swatted me away. "Go after him. I'll be okay."

"I'm not leaving you."

"Dammit, Miranda, the bastard's escaping!"

"Let him."

"No!" He tried to raise himself.

"You stay put!"

"Then go!"

Reluctantly, I rose and plunged ahead. The board-walk became a dirt trail that soon brought me into the clearing of Hobbamock's Homesite. Deserted. But Basile could be hiding inside a bark-covered *wetu*. I started for the largest one. Behind me, I heard a scraping noise, then curses. I ran toward Eel River Pond at the clearing's edge.

A clump of trees overlooked the pond. My foot slipped on a huge exposed root. I grabbed a branch to steady myself. Below, at the water's edge, Basile struggled one-handed to overturn a dugout canoe filled with water. Across the pond the lights of the Pilgrim Sands Motel winked. He'd paddle there and make his escape. My blood boiled. I had to stop him.

Wounded as he was, Basile still posed a threat. I needed a weapon. I dashed to the homesite and glanced frantically around. A cast-iron pot with three spiky legs hung over the remains of a fire. I seized the pot and hurried back to the pond.

Basile had heaved the canoe onto its side. Water sloshed out. I hadn't a second to spare. I charged him with the pot. He shoved the canoe at me. The rim caught my shins. I staggered backward, slipped on leaves, and landed hard on my rear. The pot tumbled from my hands.

I'd barely scrambled to my feet when Basile swung at me with the canoe paddle. It struck my shoulder like a white-hot anvil. Another whack seared my chest. I reeled backward, ducking when I could, taking blows when I couldn't. Basile was relentless. He wouldn't stop till he'd beaten me to jelly. I sank to my knees, scrabbling in the dirt and fallen leaves for the pot. My fingers closed on the handle. The next instant, a savage blow sent me sprawling. Bruised and battered, I could've given up, let him bludgeon me into oblivion. But I clung to the metal handle, a thin, hard line of hope. Basile swung. I rolled away, dragged the pot to me, and pulled myself into a crouch.

He loomed over me, a giant with an enormous upraised club. The club swept downward with a whoosh. I sprang forward and rammed him in the groin with the pot's spiky legs. He lurched backward. Carried forward by my own momentum, I crashed into him. We went down like dominoes, one on top of the other with the pot between us.

The rim pressed painfully into my chest. But compared to Basile, I had it easy. He squirmed beneath me, impaled by the pot's cast-iron spikes and by the arrow, whose head had sunk into the ground. Basile's face was a quivering mask of agony. His eyes pleaded for relief. Then abruptly his gaze shifted to something beyond me and stayed there, horror-struck.

My neck snapped around. I stared into the barrel of Basile's gun. Arms stretched taut as rubber bands, Caroline gripped the gun with both hands. I barely recognized her. Her strawberry blonde hair was tangled and wild. Her face was so white that I imagined her freckles had retracted into her skin. A cold fury burned in her eyes.

I hoisted myself off Basile. The pot bobbed slightly but remained embedded in him. He struggled to raise himself on his elbows.

"Don't even think about it," Caroline said between clenched teeth.

Basile sank back. He grunted and closed his eyes, a beaten bloodhound in the first gray light of dawn.

29

". . . the wind coming fair, and having a light moon, we set out at evening and, through the goodness of God, came safely home before noon the day following." Mourt's Relation

"I have a confession to make."

Startled, I glanced at Martin, seated next to me in my Peugeot. It was Sunday morning and we were on our way to Plimoth Plantation to pick up Caroline's car. Except to question me about the story I'd given the police, Martin hadn't spoken much.

Now he said, "All these years, I've blamed you for that rat's death when in fact I never cared a bit about Lotus. I only took her because Pris insisted. It was a big relief when I went away to college and could turn her over to you. When she died, I wasn't sorry."

I wagged my head in a scolding way. "You sure took your time letting me know."

"True," Martin admitted. "But as your big brother I needed something I could hold over you to keep you in line. You were such a stubborn one."

"And you were a big boss!" I retorted. I waited for his comeback, expecting this exchange to escalate into a full-fledged wrangle as had often happened in childhood and more recently as well.

Martin glanced at his lap, now free of his computer. A smile tugged at the corners of his mouth. "Maybe so," he acknowledged.

"What about Pris?" I asked, taking advantage of Martin's new forthrightness. "Still wish you'd married her instead?"

Martin shook his head. "Guess I'm just another foolish midlife male trying to recapture his youth." He stroked his Adam's apple. "But it's hard not to have at least a few regrets. Know what I mean?"

I did indeed. I could think of several other middle-aged people who were regret-ridden. Seth Lowe, for one. He'd married his dream girl only to have the dream turn sour. Then when he'd found a woman who not only loved him, but shared his passion for the past and Plimoth Plantation, he'd lost her for good.

Conor, for another. He'd spent twenty-odd years on the run. He'd taken a new name but stopped short of reinventing himself like other fugitives, who had married, raised families, and become pillars of their communities. Not Conor. He seemed to have remained frozen in flight—too frightened to connect with anyone except Beryl.

And me. One disappointment in love and I'd retreated into a safe, but passionless marriage. When it ended, I'd withdrawn into my work, content to live vicariously until the real world caught up with me.

Now that the high drama was over, I was tempted to slink back to the sidelines. Easier that than try to work things out with Nate. He'd been cool and distant at the police station, insisting he was all right and brushing off my suggestions he see a doctor. Maybe he, too, was having second thoughts. We were such different people and perhaps, after all, our differences were irreconcilable.

"One thing I've realized in the past few days," Martin went on, "is how important my family is to me. If anything had happened to Caroline—" Tears welled in his eyes. "You rescued her, Miranda. I'll never forget that as long as I live!"

He squeezed my arm. The car swerved. "I'm pulling over," I said.

When we were safely off the road, my brother did something he hadn't done since we were kids. He hugged me.

The knock on the door took me by surprise. I was down on my hands and knees, scrabbling under the futon couch for a small yellow object that turned out to be a Smiley Face ring. Slipping it on my pinky, I went to the door.

Seth Lowe stood awkwardly in the doorway, holding a kennel cab. His eyes watered and he sniffled. Ichabod Crane with a cold. "Is Caroline still here?" he asked.

"No, she and her parents left for the airport about twenty minutes ago."

"Well, in that case. . . ." He turned and started to shuffle across the grass, an old man suddenly.

My heart went out to him. "Seth," I called, "what's this about? Maybe I can help."

"I don't think so," he muttered.

"Please." I led him back to the playhouse. "Tell me what the problem is," I said after we sat down.

He gestured toward the kennel at his feet. "I need to find a home for Love and I remembered Caroline was fond of the cats. I'd keep her myself but I'm allergic."

Picturing clawed furniture and fur balls in my food, I didn't offer to take Love. "I'm not a cat person either, but maybe I can help find someone."

"Oh God!" Lowe cried abruptly, tearing at his shock of gray hair. "I can't deal with this."

"We'll find a home for her," I insisted. But Lowe seemed not to hear me. He went on tearing his hair and I realized it wasn't the cat he couldn't deal with.

I patted his arm. "I'm so sorry, Seth. I'll miss Beryl, too."

"If only I could've told her it didn't matter, didn't change a thing!"

I stared at him, bewildered. "Excuse me?"

"Like Nan, Beryl had a dark shadow in her past. She wouldn't tell me what it was, only that I'd be making a big mistake by divorcing Nan and marrying her."

"Beryl's father didn't. . . ." I left the thought unfinished. It would have been too much of a cruel coincidence for Seth to have fallen in love with another woman whose father had abused her.

"No, no," Seth said hastily. "Beryl's father was a drunken brute who beat his wife. One night when she couldn't take it anymore, Beryl's mother killed him."

"In self-defense?"

"No. She went at him with an ax while he was sleeping off a drunk. She was hanged for her crime."

Like a long-buried childhood rhyme, a phrase leaped to mind. "Hatchet dead, poor dad," I blurted.

"What?" It was Lowe's turn to stare at me in bewilderment.

"It's from McCarthy's notes for the trivia game. He used the story of John Oldham's murder by Indians to hint at Beryl's mother's crime."

"So he had something on her, too." Lowe shook his head with disgust. "What a despicable creature he was!"

"Yes, but the irony is that while he was busy digging up dirt on everyone around him, he should've been watching his own back."

Lowe said nothing, again lost in his own train of thought. "If I'd only known sooner, I could have assured her that—"

"When did you find out?"

"This morning. From Conor." His eyes filled with tears and he tore at his hair.

"Seth," I murmured sympathetically. Love let out a plaintive meow. Lowe reached for the kennel cab and stood up. Love's whiskered face stared at me from behind the bars. Too bad Caroline was gone because she would have given this orphan a home. She was attached to the cats, especially Love, the shy one. She'd told me how Love had curled purring in her lap on Friday night, comforting her while Beryl told her hard truths about Conor.

"I'll take the cat," I said impulsively.

Lowe sneezed. "But I thought you said you didn't care for cats."

"I've changed my mind. Please let me keep her."

Lowe put down the kennel cab. "Thank you, Miranda." He wiped his eyes. "I'm sorry you and Caroline got dragged into this awful business. Conor is, too. He's staying with me now, while he gets some things," Lowe paused, choosing his words carefully, "sorted out.   He intended to go to the village Friday night. But first he wanted to see for himself what had happened to Beryl. At her house, he got into an argument with the police, who were ready to arrest me for her murder."

"We managed okay without him," I said.

"Thank heaven for that."

"Has Nan turned up?" I asked after a moment.

"She's at her sister's in Duxbury. That's where she went Friday night. And where I expect she'll remain," he muttered without looking at me.

After Lowe had gone, I completed my check of the playhouse, unearthing a Cat-in-the-Hat tee shirt and a Kermit the Frog toothbrush. Caroline's little-kid stuff. Would she cling to it, or make the leap to adulthood?

I suspected the latter. She'd remained calm and in control when she made her statement to the police and dealt with her frantic parents. Martin and Eileen were a bit in awe of her, especially after they heard how she'd held a gun on Basile until the police arrived.

I packed the little-kid stuff in a plastic bag anyway, picked up the kennel cab, and left the playhouse. Love crouched in the carrier, balancing like a child on a skateboard as I brought her to my car. After I'd slid the carrier onto the backseat, she pressed her face against the metal grate and howled in protest.

"Look, Love, I'm not sure how this is going to work out either, but we'll just have to make the best of it."

"Miranda?"

Nate stood behind me, baseball hat pulled down over his forehead so that only a tiny strip of bandage was visible, eyes hidden by reflector sunglasses. I felt tentative and awkward, almost as if we were meeting for the first time.

"I'm glad you're still here," he said. "I would've called, but I figured you were tied up with your family."

A likely excuse, I thought.   But then again, maybe there was some truth to it. I remembered how he'd stood apart at the police station while Martin and Eileen swarmed around Caroline and me, crying, laughing, and embracing us. When I finally introduced Nate to Martin and Eileen, I observed Martin sizing him up. Martin had always been critical of my friends, especially boyfriends, though he and Simon had gotten along fine. *Who's this guy and what's going on between him and my kid sister?* I imagined him thinking. My halting and incomplete explanations didn't help matters either. No wonder Martin withheld the stamp of elder sibling approval. Or that Nate felt shut out. "I would've called, too, but. . . ." I shrugged, uncertain what to say.

Nate brushed a leaf off the top of my car. "Headed back to Cambridge?"

I nodded.

"I'm going away myself."

"Oh?"

"Deer week starts at dawn tomorrow. I'm leaving with a couple of buddies to camp out in the woods in western Mass."

Meeting, then parting, I thought with a pang. What should I say? Have a nice time and a nice life? Instead I said more stiffly than I would've liked, "I'm glad you came by because I never really thanked you for what you did Friday night."

Nate shifted his weight from one foot to the other. "If I'd had my rifle instead of my bow and arrow, that bastard would be pushing up daisies instead of lolling in a hospital bed."

"He *is* in critical condition."

"Still. . . ." Nate studied a crack in the sidewalk. "That stuff about your family coming over on the *Fortune*— I was a fool to react the way I did."

"And I should've known better than to blurt it out just then."

Nate removed his sunglasses and looked at me. "I don't have to leave right away."

"Me either."

"Well then."

"Mrr—ow!"

"What've you got there?" Nate peered into the backseat.

"My new cat, L—"

"I know. Just wanted to hear you say it again."
Nate's brown-black eyes brimmed with laughter.

"You!" I punched his arm playfully.

"No, *you*." He drew me to him and this time neither
of us held back.